Gabe

PRAISE FOR THE WORKS OF M. MALONE

"I am now officially in love with the Alexander family."
--*Smitten by Reading (Grade: A-) on One More Day*

"Malone has a winner with The Alexanders series! Please keep them coming!"
--*Joyfully Reviewed on One More Day*

"Nicholas is perfect leading man material..."
-- *4 stars, Romance Junkies on The Things I Do for You*

"Malone gives her reader a story full of smart dialogue, compelling characters, and a strong story-line. The Alexanders and their friends will draw you in and keep you coming back for more."
-- *4 stars, Romantic Reads on He's the Man*

This book has angst, humor, sexy times, and love. What more could you ask for? I hope there are going to be more in this series and you can bet I will be first in line.
-- *4 $^{1/2}$ stars, S.W. & More Book Reviews on He's the Man*

Titles by M. Malone

BLUE-COLLAR BILLIONAIRES

Available Now
TANK
FINN
GABE

Future Books
ZACK
LUKE

THE ALEXANDERS

Available Now
One More Day
The Things I Do for You
He's the Man
All I Need is You
Say You Will

Future Books
Just One Thing

Gabe

BLUE-COLLAR BILLIONAIRES #3

M. Malone

Chapter One

Sasha

Two months earlier...

"Five minutes, Sasha."

The words from the set director race through me, leaving a string of nerves that feel like live wires. I roll my head and turn back to the mirror, scrutinizing every aspect of my appearance. A costume would have felt over the top, so instead I chose to wear a black cocktail dress with a flirty hem and delicate cap sleeves. My makeup is minimal and I've pulled my ultra-curly black hair up into an elegant knot on the top of my head. My skin glows despite the harsh lighting backstage.

Everything I've done the past year has led me to this moment. Networking, auditioning and finally being chosen to appear on the show *SuperNova*, a televised competition to win a recording contract, has been the culmination of a lifelong dream. I have worked so hard and sacrificed so much.

My hand shakes as I reapply my lip gloss. Chaz's earlier words run through my mind.

All you care about is this stupid competition.

Do you seriously think you have a chance?

You're not good enough.

You're nobody.

I shake my head to dispel the negative thoughts and rub my thumb below my lip to catch a stray bit of color. Then I leave the dressing area and walk to the left-side stage entrance. It's true that I've sacrificed a lot for this, including time with family and friends, but I'm ashamed to realize how little my boyfriend actually thought of my dreams. How little he believed in me. All the time I'd spent with him trying to make up for the long hours rehearsing and the Saturday nights when I couldn't go out because I was performing, would have been better spent with my parents or my sisters.

I take a deep breath and place a shaky hand against my lower belly. The muscles clench beneath my fingers and I suck in another breath as I listen to the roar of the crowd. Despite the sudden attack of nerves, competing on a major show like *SuperNova* is everything I've ever dreamed of. I've been performing in clubs and coffeehouses for years all with the same goal: to end up having a chance like the one I have right now. I won't let personal issues derail the most exciting thing that has ever happened to me.

"Miss Whitman, you're up next."

A harried backstage attendant hands me a microphone and then hustles away before I can respond. Another contestant smiles at me before peeking around the curtain. The man with her strokes her cheek and she buries her face against his shoulder. My eyes burn watching the loving embrace. Chaz was supposed to be here with me, supporting me, but now I'm alone with his last words to me ringing in my head.

You're nobody.

I shake off the negative thoughts when I hear my name being called. Head held high, I step out from behind the curtain.

* * * * *

Present Day

"Being a godmother is awesome."

I hold out my arms and my best friend's one-year-old daughter, Hope, crawls obligingly into my lap. She's the mirror image of Kaylee, especially her big, dark eyes. Holding her always gives me a sharp stab of envy. I've always loved kids and wanted a big family.

Unfortunately I'd need to be able to pick out a half-decent guy in order to make that happen.

Kay's future in-laws brought their kids and they're all running around the backyard of her new house. By the sound of their happy shrieks and squeals, they're having a ball. Hope looks over my shoulder at a particularly loud scream right near the window of the living room where we're sitting.

"You'll be running around with the big kids before long too, sweetie." I snuggle my face into her soft, dark curls and inhale that perfect baby smell. Until I can get my own personal life sorted, I'll indulge my need for snuggles with Hope.

Kay bites the top of a package of cookies, trying to pull it open with her teeth. "Thank you for bringing me cookies. You are the best godmother ever. And the best friend ever."

At her words, I reach over and squeeze her hand. I've been right there by Kay's side ever since she got pregnant by the douchebag ex-boyfriend who promptly ditched her, so I know how hard things were for her in the beginning. Her parents are just as conservative as mine so she was hit with a double whammy of parental guilt and the shame of being an unwed mother who suddenly couldn't show her face in church.

I wanted nothing more than to track that guy down and rearrange a few body parts but Kay is such a softie. She doesn't like violence or harsh words. What she needed most from me was support. So I had to put my homicidal urges on hold so I could be there while she dealt with being pregnant and suddenly having a child to support. Luckily it wasn't too long before she met her fiancé. Kay is a singer just like I am, except she's got the kind of voice that sends chills up and down your spine. A local producer took her under his wing and she ended up falling in love with his older brother.

As if on cue, Elliott Alexander sticks his head into the room. He's a gruff, no-nonsense kind of guy with big muscular arms and a permanently brooding expression. In other words, the last person I would have expected my sweet friend to end up with. But there's no denying the way he feels about her. His dark eyes immediately laser in on Kay.

"Are you okay, baby?"

Kay grins up at him. "I'm fine. And you're supposed to be meeting Nick today, aren't you?"

He walks into the room, his eyes running over her. The heated looks between these two make me want to open another window. If we weren't such good friends, I would be completely sick with envy every time I looked at Kay. She has everything I've ever wanted. A recording contract, a man who looks at her like she's his oxygen and a sweet little girl.

I cuddle Hope a little closer. These types of feelings make me feel like such a jerk. Kay has always been my biggest cheerleader and she deserves every bit of her good fortune.

"Hey Eli. You can't bear to let Kay out of your sight for even one afternoon, huh?"

Eli grunts but the corners of his lips turn up slightly. When we first met I was completely intimidated by him but after witnessing how the big, strong guy turns to absolute mush at one word from my best friend, I know his gruff looks are just a mask. He's one of the good guys.

"Hey, Sasha. I'm glad you're here."

"Eli, I'm fine. Don't keep your brother waiting." Kay sounds completely exasperated so I have a feeling this is a familiar argument. Even though I'm jealous of the way Eli looks at her, I'm not sure I could deal with that type of alpha male. That much attention at once could be exhausting.

"I'm going. Put your feet up," Eli orders and then kisses Kay on the forehead.

Once he's gone, Kay immediately sits back up and grabs the package of cookies again. "So what's been going on with you? Dating anyone new?"

"I'm not dating."

At that blunt statement, Kay looks over at me sharply. "Since when? Have you taken some religious vow that I'm unaware of or something?"

"Let's just say I'm on hiatus. I have a knack for picking the wrong guys so I think staying single is the best thing I can do for myself right now."

Kay purses her lips. I know this look. She's trying to figure out how to tell me that she disagrees without hurting my feelings. "That seems a little drastic. You just need to meet the right guy. Eli could introduce you to some of the guys who work for him."

"I don't think a set up is the answer. When I'm ready I'll start dating again."

"No offense sweetie, but you have broken radar when it comes to men. It's time you let someone else choose for you. I was actually

6

going to try to fix you up with Tank before he started dating Emma," she says, mentioning one of Eli's employees.

"The fact that you were thinking of putting us together proves my point. *Setups never work.* Tank and I didn't even like each other at first." Even though I've always thought Tank was sexy in a dangerous sort of way, we didn't exactly hit it off when we met. Probably because he suspected me of stalking Kay and manhandled me a few times.

Kay crunches on another cookie. "My point is that he's exactly the type of guy you need. One that Eli has done a background check on so you know what you're getting into. What about Tank's brother?"

I shake my head. "Finn is engaged, remember? Emma invited you guys to the surprise engagement party she's throwing for him."

She gives me a knowing look. "Not him. The brother he asked Eli to find. Luke? I've seen his picture and he is a cutie."

Dang. I was hoping to throw her off but I guess she's already heard about Tank finding some long-lost family members. Kay doesn't know that I've met Luke before.

"He's some sort of computer genius. He's also young. *Really young.*" I'm hoping she'll stop asking questions about Luke. She can be like a dog with a bone sometimes when she gets an idea in her head.

Kay rolls her eyes. "He's our age, I'm pretty sure. Early twenties."

"Really?" I actually hadn't known that part but knowing Kay

she snooped and looked at the background check Eli did on him. "He looks like a baby. You know I like my men a little more mature than that."

"I guess I can't argue with that."

Kay definitely understands how I feel on that score since her fiancé is about a decade older than we are.

"You know how people do those cleanse diets? Well, that's what I need for my dating life. I'm on the stay single plan. A man fast!"

Kay doesn't look impressed.

"Well, whenever you get tired of your man-less diet, I'm sure I can set you up with one of Eli's cousins or something. As fine as the Alexander boys are, you know there have to be some hot cousins on that family tree somewhere."

By the excitement in her voice, I know she's not going to let this go. So I just nod and then try to think of something, anything, to distract her.

"You're still coming to the engagement party right?" It's hard to believe that it'll be here so soon. When Emma found out that I was opening a small business, she asked Finn to introduce me to some local business owners. This party is going to be a networking dream. I'm excited but also nervous.

"Yeah, we'll be there. Eli has gotten to know Finn pretty well lately. It's good for him to get some guy time in. It'll be good for you, too. You've been holed up so long ever since the show—"

"No talking about that day! You know the rules."

"Sasha, it's really not that bad. I saw the video—"

"Kay!"

She looks a little scared, probably because of the death glare I'm giving her. "I'm just saying that you've cut yourself off from the world for the last two months. Yes, whoever uploaded that video to Youtube is a jerk but you can't let this keep you from living your life."

She stops talking and sits back with a disgruntled look on her face when I make a cutting motion with my hand across my neck. "Okay, okay, no talking about it. I'm just saying it's *not that big of a deal.*"

"Everything is going to be fine." I don't look at Kay, trying to keep a lid on my emotions.

After my disastrous appearance on the reality TV show, *SuperNova,* I had retreated from my life for a while. I'd known that going on the show had been a long shot but I'd assumed that I'd get some publicity. Several of the past contestants so far had been offered recording contracts even if they didn't win.

I'd been so sure that I could impress the judges and walk away with a contract, a career, anything other than the heaping dose of humiliation I'd gotten from choking on stage on live television.

"I know you've been worried about me but you don't have to be. My whole family is investing in my new venture and I think this is going to be the start of something wonderful. For all of us."

I lift Hope up in the air and nuzzle her belly, prompting a round of charming giggles from her.

Kay's eyes are shining. "I'm so proud of you, Sasha. I know

everyone in the community is excited about having our own jazz club. Eli's cousin, the one who's a reporter, will be there. I'm sure you'll be in the newspaper. And all the other local business owners are going to be out to support you. This is the perfect opportunity for you to meet someone new."

I'm about to protest again when Kay reaches out and grabs my hand. "I know you don't want to. I know you think it's a waste of time. But honey, that's just because you're so used to bad guys. There are some amazing men out there. I got lucky enough to find one of them and I just want the same for you. You deserve that."

I close my eyes and let the feeling of contentment wash over me. Kay and I have been friends since elementary school and I've never had a friend who has supported me the way she does. No matter how many times I fail, no matter how many stupid decisions I make, she always believes the best in me.

When I open my eyes, ready to agree just to make her feel better, I smile at the sight before me. Kay is snuggled into the pillows of the couch, her hand that's encased in mine completely slack.

She's fast asleep.

I pick up Hope and snuggle her against my shoulder. "Come on sweetie, let's go for a walk and let Mommy have a nap."

And hopefully when Kay wakes up, she'll have forgotten all about her plan to fix me up.

Chapter Two

Gabe

There are many things that I'm willing to do for family. Several things cross my mind that I've done in the past, things I'm not particularly proud of and that are one foot over the line into illegal territory. But as I listen to my brother Zack, I'm seriously considering rethinking my stance on family loyalty.

"She's a friend of Emma's. Finn wants me to help her with setting up her business. Mentoring if you will," Zack explains.

"So let me see if I understand correctly. Finn asks you for a favor and you want to pawn it off on me? Nice."

Zack chuckles. "Oh come on. You know I'm not good with shit like this. You're the one who handles the customers at the shop. It shouldn't take that long, maybe a few afternoons explaining how to get started. Showing her the paperwork she needs to file. You know, stuff like that."

I shift my cell phone to my other shoulder. "Do you really think I'm the best person to be a mentor? Wouldn't she be more comfortable with someone she knows? And why the hell didn't Finn ask *me* to do it?"

Zack snorts. "He knows how you are with women. I'm sure he doesn't want his female friends anywhere near you. Look, he's going to set up a meeting but I figure I can just claim to be sick and send you in my place. Finn won't know until after the fact."

I groan and look impatiently to the long ass line I've been standing in for what feels like forever. Zack is lucky he caught me when I'm feeling generous. Whoever this poor girl is, if I don't agree, she's going to have to suffer through an afternoon with Zack grunting and scowling. Standing in the local business office reminds me of when I was first starting out and had no one to help me. The least I can do is pay it forward, especially to help out a friend of a friend.

"Ok, I'll do it. But I'm only committing to a few days and then after that she's on her own."

"Awesome. I'll let Finn know to set up the meeting. Thanks. I'll owe you one."

I hang up and slip my cell phone back into the inner pocket of my suit jacket. Today I've dressed the part in a simple two-button pinstripe that never fails to convey responsible business owner.

The auto garage that Zack and I own has been doing really well for a few years now. He's been trying to convince me to open another location for six months. Since most of the counties in Virginia require you to appear in person to gain a business license, I've been putting it off. But after running reports and seeing the proof in black and white that our business has been on a steady increase for the past year, I finally agreed.

But as the voices of the women in front of me increase, so does my feeling that I should have waited longer to tackle this particular issue. Preferably when we were big enough to be a corporation and I could designate someone else to handle these sorts of things.

"This is the wrong form. You need an application for a business license, not a liquor license."

The woman behind the counter looks like she's rapidly losing patience. With her gray hair and oversized glasses, she reminds me of a teacher I once had. If this lady is anything like Miss Rosings, then all the explanations in the world aren't going to cut it.

The girl at the counter is apparently fearless. Or reckless. Her voice rises in what is starting to sound like hysteria.

"But that can't be right! The last time I was here, the man told me I needed a liquor license. I downloaded all this and filled it out and now you're telling me this is wrong again?"

"Ma'am, you do need a liquor license. This is just the wrong place to submit that. This is where you get your business license. Did you bring the form for that?"

"No, I thought this was what I needed."

The Miss Rosings lookalike hands a sheaf of forms over the desk. "Fill those out and then bring them back. Next!"

"But wait a minute—"

"Next!"

I can feel the tension rising in the room. This is the last time I volunteer to handle the paperwork just to spare Zack. Normally we share the administrative hassles but I wanted to escape the office. When I made the decision a few years back to go straight, I knew I'd have to get used to a more sedate life. Being a responsible law-abiding citizen is by definition less exciting but it's also safer. There's no worries about who might be after me or whether I'll get caught up in something. And I'm proud of the atmosphere Zack and I have created at the shop. We have fun most of the time.

We have a great group of guys and Jim and the crew are like family. But every day it's the same thing. Every night it's the same thing. Sometimes the need for excitement has me feeling like I want to crawl out of my skin. Or scream.

More than anything I just want something to surprise me.

The guy in front of me makes a frustrated noise and puts his hands on his head. I can't see much of the girl at the counter, just a riot of long black curls and an oversized black coat. But she doesn't look like she's going anywhere.

I lean forward. "Sweetheart, you're holding up the line."

"*Did you just call me sweetheart?*" She whips around and the rest of whatever else I was about to say gets trapped in the back of my throat.

14

Golden brown skin. Full, pouty lips. Whiskey-colored eyes framed by long lashes. Big innocent eyes. She looks like Bambi. From her husky voice I was expecting a much older woman, not this fiery little thing who is currently shooting daggers at me with her eyes.

Now *this* is a surprise.

By the time my brain makes sense of what she's said, I open my mouth to say something and nothing comes out. While she's distracted, the guy in front of me pushes past and drops a big file folder on the counter. Bambi looks over at him and then sends me another glare. Then she clutches the papers to her chest and walks out, the glass door to the office swinging shut behind her. A sheet of paper floats behind her and lands in the hallway.

I glance up front again at the guy's overflowing folder. Then I turn and walk out, pausing only to pick up the piece of paper she dropped. I read the top of the form. *Virginia Alcoholic Beverage Control.* It's an application for a liquor license, filled out with her name, business name, address—the works. *Sasha Whitman.* The dramatic swipe of her signature fits her.

My hand clenches around the form. Although it's doubtful she'll thank me, I follow her outside. I definitely don't want anyone else to pick this up. Any psycho could have found this. Or a guy like me which isn't much better.

I jog slightly to catch up with her in the parking lot. She's bent over, shoving her things onto the passenger seat of an ancient Volvo. I wince when she closes the door and it lets out a screeching sound. When she turns around, I'm startled at the tear tracks on her face.

She wipes at them hastily with the back of her hand.

"Please tell me I didn't make you cry."

That coaxes a small smile from her lips. "No, it wasn't you. In case you couldn't tell I'm having a fantastic day."

"Well, good. I honestly wasn't trying to be patronizing. I was trying to warn you not to provoke the warden in there. She doesn't look like the sympathetic type."

"Yeah, I noticed." Her words aren't even bitter, more resigned. She seems sad now.

I hold out the paper she dropped. "You'll need this. It needs to be submitted at the ABC. You can mail it though. You only have to appear in person for the business license."

"Really?" She takes the paper hesitantly. "Thank you. This whole thing is so confusing and I feel like I'm doing it all wrong. Probably because I am."

"I could look over your forms for you. I know a bit about owning a small business. I can probably save you from the most obvious mistakes."

It doesn't escape my notice that I'm volunteering to help her when Zack had to beg me to do this for Finn's friend. The universe must be rewarding me because I'll definitely tutor Bambi in anything she wants to learn.

She looks doubtful. "I don't even know you."

"Not to point out the obvious but I've already seen all your information. If I was a stalker, I wouldn't have given that back."

Her laugh animates her entire face, making her eyes sparkle. "I suppose that's true. But just because you aren't a stalker doesn't mean you aren't trouble. And I've had enough of trouble."

She turns to go again and I'm suddenly gripped with panic. I don't know what's come over me but I can't just let her leave.

"Trouble can be fun." I give her my most charming smile, the one that Zack calls the moneymaker. "Give me a chance to prove that."

She sighs, the sound so weary that it should be coming from someone three times her age.

"You don't need to prove anything Calvin Klein. I can see right through you. I can probably tell you what you ate for breakfast."

She crosses her arms and looks up at me, her eyes fixed on my face. "You're gorgeous and you know you are. It's something you use to your advantage. But there are times when it's not to your advantage so you try to tone it down, such as with those glasses you're wearing."

Stunned, my hand reaches up to touch the clear frames I wore this morning to make myself look older. It's something I only do when I need to appear on behalf of the business.

"I bet you don't even wear glasses," she continues. "A guy with cheekbones like yours wouldn't want anything obscuring the view of his perfect face. I bet you had laser eye surgery and you just wear those glasses because they make you look intellectual. They also save you from the envy of men around you because they'll either dismiss you as a nerdy type or assume that you're gay and not their competition."

I stand as she neatly dissects me, ticking off each point on her fingers.

"I've dated pretty men like you before so I've already seen this show. I'm not impressed by flattery or whatever line you're currently thinking up. You're probably not even listening right now because you're thinking of how to sweet talk me."

I'm stunned again because she's right. In the middle of her rant, I was only half paying attention because I was trying to think of what to say to calm her down. As I stand in front of her, the entirety of who I am exposed as if she'd ripped my seams open, I can't think of a single thing to say in my own defense.

"Goodbye, pretty boy." She rounds the car and climbs behind the wheel while I stand gaping at her. Once inside, she puts on her seat belt and then pulls out slowly. I watch until her taillights turn right on the main road and she disappears.

Once she's gone, I'm able to clear the cobwebs from my brain and suddenly I can move again. What the hell was that? I let out a breath and turn in circles, looking around the parking lot as if the asphalt can give me answers.

The first time I meet a woman who can see past all of my bullshit and she wants nothing to do with me.

* * * * *

I am a good guy.

I remind myself of that fact as I drive to meet my brother at our father's hotel, the StarCrest. Getting dressed down by a pint-sized girl with innocent eyes shouldn't have shaken me this much but I can't help it. She took one look at me and instantly saw everything that I've worked so hard to hide.

I've spent a lot of time training myself to hide my roots and to appear the way a responsible local businessman should. I help little old ladies cross the street. I recycle. I make a number of charitable contributions each year. Anyone looking at me will see a solid, respectable, upstanding member of the community.

Which is *exactly* what I want them to see.

As I pull up in front of the hotel, I lift my hand and wave to Zack, who is leaning casually against the side of the building. When I step out of the car, a valet appears instantly. His lips curl up into a grin of appreciation as he takes in the restored 1967 Chevy Corvette. As he takes the keys and the twenty dollar bill in my hand, I slap him on the back. "Take care of my girlfriend for me."

Zack rebuilt the engine for me and the leather seats and exterior have all been painstakingly restored. I've spent more money on this car than most guys would spend on an engagement ring. Hell, I love this car and since the 400 hp under the engine practically gives me a hard-on every time I slide behind the wheel, this is the closest thing to a long-term relationship I've ever had.

"Yes, sir!"

As I move back, my eyes land on a man across the street. He's too far away to see clearly but I know what I'll see if I get closer. He has a thin white scar across his cheek. This is the second time I've seen this guy. The valet is waiting patiently so I move out of the way and meet Zack in front of the doors leading into the elegant lobby.

As we walk across the polished marble floors, Zack peers at me with a concerned expression. "Are you sure you're ready for this?"

Although his question is annoying, it's an honor since I know that I'm one of the few things in the world that my brother gives two fucks about.

"I'm fine. We decided this is the best way so we'll stick to the plan."

Zack doesn't look convinced, which just serves to remind me of all the things that I've been trying to forget all week. That I'm breaking a promise I made to myself years ago. That what I'm about to do is unethical, possibly even illegal, and most importantly, just *wrong*.

But knowing that I should feel guilty for what I'm about to do doesn't change anything. Neither does the very real possibility of failure. I'm about to pull my first con in years and I'm excited.

After all, it's not every day you pull a job on your own father.

We enter the elevator and I'm glad there's no one else getting on. I need a few moments of peace before I have to turn it "on." That's how I think of it. Like a game. Manipulating people into doing what you want — whether it's to give you money, access or information— is about making them feel that you're on their side. That you're their friend. It's completely mental. It's a rush but it's also exhausting and requires one hundred percent of my concentration and focus. And what we're doing today is too important for me to risk screwing up because I'm shredded with second thoughts and guilt.

My father has come back into our lives offering money and apologies but very little in the way of explanations. Nothing to explain why he left our mothers pregnant and alone and nothing to explain why he hasn't contacted us before. For a little while it's been like a dream come true but I'm too cynical to believe that anything is free.

Maxwell Marshall has his reasons for coming back into our lives now and I plan to find out what they are.

"Do you have time to help me with an engine rebuild later today?"

Zack apparently doesn't share my need for self-reflection. The sides of his hair have grown in a little and the top is spiked up into a little mini-hawk. He's wearing a short-sleeved shirt so all his ink is exposed. Our reflection in the mirrored elevator doors is pretty amusing. He looks like he's on the verge of committing a felony and I look like I'm on the way to a business meeting.

How deceiving appearances can be.

"I don't have time today. Maybe tomorrow?"

Zack makes a face. "On a Friday night? Aren't you going to be busy?"

I don't look up but I can sense his scrutiny. "No."

"What happened to Gabriella? The two of you were so cute together. Even your names were cute."

I snort as the elevator opens on the top floor with a tinny *ding*. Zack never liked Gabriella. Not that it mattered since I wasn't inviting her over for family dinners.

21

"We parted amicably."

He shrugs and follows me down the hall. "Which means she begged you to stay and you convinced her the whole breakup was her idea, right?"

Gabriella was a way to pass the time and I suspect I was the same for her. There were no tears when we broke up. She just seemed more annoyed that she would have to find someone else for the occasional night of dinner and uncomplicated sex. I suspect she was more upset about the disruption to her schedule than she was about the possibility of not seeing me again.

Zack knocks on the door of my father's suite before I have a chance to. I don't bother giving him an answer and he doesn't look like he's expecting one anyway. Probably because he already knows he's right.

Sometimes I hate that he knows me so well.

There's movement behind the door, a soft shuffling and then the sound of voices. The door opens and Carol, one of my father's many assistants, stands in the doorway. She's a pretty young redhead with soft blue eyes and a perky ass. My father has managed to surround himself with beautiful women even in his retirement. He particularly seems to like redheads.

Carol stands back so we can enter. "Zack. Gabe. Your father is expecting you. Please come in."

"Last chance to back out," Zack murmurs.

He glances back at me and I nod. He looks vaguely disappointed but then he turns back and steps across the threshold. Carol smiles at him absently but when her eyes meet mine, she blushes slightly and looks away. I sigh.

The game is on.

* * * * *

When we enter the room, Max turns toward us. If he's surprised to see that Zack is with me, he doesn't let on. Part of our unholy deal with our newly found billionaire pops is that we each have to visit him for an hour each week. Zack has already been to see him at his usual time yesterday. My brother is here today for a different purpose.

Today, he's the distraction.

"Hey Max. Taken over the world yet?"

It's a familiar joke by now, spawned by the fact that my father owns so many different businesses. There are few industries that he doesn't have some interests in and as someone who grew up owning jack shit, the concept is fascinating to me.

"Not yet. There's always tomorrow." His familiar reply comes in a voice that sounds raspier than usual. He's sitting in a chair by the window but his wheelchair is in the corner. I wonder how hard he had to fight to be allowed to sit unaided.

Zack takes a seat on the couch, looking uncomfortable. It's been a long time since he's done this and that's why I only tapped him for an easy role today. Manipulating doesn't come easily to Zack and he's only doing this because we both agreed that it's time for us to find out what our father is up to. Zack never enjoyed these games the way I did. But then I've always known that my little brother is a much better person than I am.

"Here you go. A Coke for you and a glass of water." Carol brings the drinks in on a tray, the same way she always does. Somehow she manages to keep straight all of our usual drink orders, something Zack and I realized during our planning.

He looks up at me and nods slightly. Then he reaches forward and knocks the glass of Coke over, the dark liquid immediately spreading across the coffee table. Carol gasps and jumps back.

That's my cue.

"Here, use my handkerchief." I step closer, much closer, into her personal space.

She looks up at me, her pupils dilating slightly. When she realizes how close I am, she sucks in a breath and her cheeks flush red. I'm using the fact that she likes me to my advantage, something I should feel terrible about. Instead, I raise the white handkerchief I brought for this purpose in front of her face.

As soon as her eyes latch onto it, I move a little closer, bumping into her. My right hand simultaneously unclips the security card on her waistband.

"Oh thank you," she whispers. She takes the small square of fabric and blots at the drops on her sleeve.

"I'll grab some towels from the bathroom."

Before Carol can respond, I duck into the hallway. The suite has three bedrooms, each with their own bathroom. I can never poke around because Carol is always there but I've observed her entering and exiting my father's private area before. That's how I know she needs an access card. Paranoid bastard. How many people have this level of security on their bedroom? But his security just increases my belief that he's hiding something. Innocent people are rarely this careful. Hopefully Zack can keep them distracted for a few minutes so I can get into my father's room.

I glance behind me but the hall is empty so I hold the card up to the door on the last room. The electronic keypad flashes green and I enter. The curtains are drawn slightly but it doesn't matter. The only thing I want to do is check out what's next to my father's bed.

We spent the last few weeks planning this and the one thing that Zack and I agreed on was that whatever Max is up to, it's personal. He's spent a lot of time and money ensuring that his children have to talk to him. But what we can't figure out is why now? Since his stroke, my father hasn't been able to get around as easily so we theorized that he'd keep his most important possessions near his bed. Where he can reach them.

I pull out my cell phone and start snapping pictures of everything around me. A spill won't distract Carol for long. After snapping everything near the bed and everything visible when I pull open the nightstand drawer, I leave the room.

A few seconds later, Carol enters the hallway from the living area. Her eyes narrow when she sees me standing in the hall.

"Did you get a towel?"

I run a hand through my hair and feign confusion. "Uh no, actually. I was looking for a linen closet and then realized that this isn't actually an apartment. It's easy to forget this is a hotel suite."

Her pinched look dissolves into a smile. "Yeah, it is. But you can just take one from any of the bathrooms. It's fine."

I duck into the guest room I'm standing next to and walk past the perfectly made up bed to the bathroom. It's fully stocked and ready for guests, so I grab two towels from the stack above the toilet.

When I come back out, I hand one to Carol. "Sorry about that again. My brother can be a little clumsy."

"Oh it's fine. He was so apologetic about it that I actually feel bad. He got more of it on himself than me. He said one of his tattoos wasn't fully healed and it was burning him. I had to help him get it off. Poor guy."

My mouth twitches. Zack is not a fan of being touched by people he doesn't know so if he had to let her play nursemaid, I'm sure I'm going to get an earful about it later.

When we enter the living room, Max looks over from his seat by the window. "Is everything okay?"

"Yeah, found 'em." I hold up the towels. His eyes follow me as I walk over to the table and make a big production about cleaning it up. I nod at Zack, letting him know that I got what I needed. He stands and walks over to Max, positioning his body between us. I pull the keycard from my pocket and tuck it under the towel.

"You don't have to do that. I can clean it up." Carol appears at my side with the other towel.

"I don't mind." I bend back to the liquid dripping onto the carpet before she can protest again.

Carol wipes the tray she brought the drinks on. As I'm mopping up the puddle on the carpet, I casually toss the keycard over to the side of the table where she's standing. When she wipes the side of the table, she stops when she spots it.

Her hand immediately flies to her waistband. "Oh I must have dropped it." Her soft mumble is barely audible over Zack's loud voice. I glance over my shoulder.

"Are you telling him about that weird tattoo artist?"

Zack looks over his shoulder at our prearranged signal. He moves out of the way so Max is visible. I stand with the soiled towel in my hands, the table behind me arranged the way it was when we arrived. Carol stands too, holding the tray with the empty glasses.

"I'll be back with more drinks."

Max watches as Carol leaves the room. Then his eyes swing back to me. For a long moment, we don't break eye contact. Of all of his children, I am probably the most like Max. We're both liars and manipulators, and extremely good at it. The only difference is that I made a conscious decision to stop. To try to be something better.

But as he watches me, there's something in his eyes I wasn't expecting. Like he knows there was more to all that chaos than meets the eye but he isn't going to call me on it. Like he's aware that I'm playing him but doesn't even care to stop it.

Something that looks a lot like regret.

"Your brother was just showing off his latest artwork. Sit down, Gabriel. And tell me what you've been up to."

Chapter Three

Sasha

"Is it ready yet?"

I look over at my sister Audra in confusion. "What?"

She points at the pan in front of me. "The cornbread. You took it out of the oven and you've just been standing here staring into space ever since."

"Sorry. I was just thinking."

I know I've been spaced out today but it's just because I've been so busy.

After spending weeks holed up in my house and avoiding the world, I'd realized that there were so many other dreams to pursue.

Before I'd gone on the show I'd made inquiries about a space for rent in downtown New Haven. It has always been a dream of mine to open a small jazz lounge and my entire family promised to invest.

After my public humiliation, I was doubly glad that I had something else to focus on. Making plans and dreaming about how to make it happen has given me a new goal and my sanity back.

I signed a lease on a commercial space in the center of town earlier this week so it's finally happening. And I can't wait to share the good news with my family.

I look up when my sister Brenna enters the kitchen with a covered casserole dish. She's only a year older than I am and we've always been close. Even though Audra's only four years older than me, growing up it felt like light years. Her tendency to be a know-it-all doesn't help.

Brenna puts her casserole dish down on the stove and then shucks off her coat. "I brought that smothered chicken casserole you like so much."

The rest of the house is suspiciously quiet. Usually my brother-in-law Evan comes to the kitchen to say hi before plopping down in front of the television. Brenna also usually has my nephew, Carter, on her hip.

"Where is everyone?"

Brenna glances over at Audra before turning to the refrigerator. "Evan stayed at home with the baby. We thought it'd be nice to have it be just us tonight. Like old times."

Something about that doesn't seem right. Audra's husband

stayed home tonight with their two daughters, too. She'd claimed they were feeling under the weather. I know how overprotective Audra can be so I didn't think it was anything serious but maybe Brenna didn't want to expose Carter to any germs she thought the girls might be carrying.

"Well, I'd hoped everyone would be here because I have good news."

Opening a small jazz lounge for enthusiasts like my father is a dream come true. There were a few times I almost gave up this past week, especially when I got to the business office and found out that I'd done my paperwork incorrectly. I had to stand in line all over again this afternoon but I've finally got it all sorted. And the feeling when my landlord gave me the keys to my new space was magical. This has been the culmination of years of saving and planning. I'm doubly excited to tell my family about it since they've all promised to invest in the club with me. It'll be a true family endeavor.

Mom enters the kitchen then and we all scurry to finish getting things ready. Once we're all seated at the table, we all clasp hands while she says grace. Brenna's casserole smells amazing. But when I pick up a serving spoon and stick it in the dish, I realize what's missing from the table.

"Where's Daddy?"

My mom doesn't meet my eyes as she answers. "He went out. Which is for the best because we need to talk to you."

"About what?" I hold out my plate to accept a serving of vegetables. Then Brenna puts a heaping serving of the casserole next it.

"The club. About our investment," Mom states.

"What is there to talk about? The grand opening should be in a few months if all goes to plan. I've already signed a lease for the space."

"Sasha, don't you think it's time to consider some alternatives? You were counting on getting publicity from being on television. But now … "

She doesn't say anything else but I can imagine what she's leaving unsaid. Now that I'm not on the show, how will the club get exposure? Now that I'm a failure and a laughingstock, who will come?

I pause with my fork halfway to my mouth. Across from me Audra chews her food slowly. When I look over at Brenna she won't look at me either.

"So you're all pulling out? How am I supposed to have my grand opening? I won't be able to afford to build out the space let alone pay for furniture or fixtures. Thank God I got Kay and Eli to invest."

Audra doesn't look impressed. "Eli owns that big security company. He can afford to lose money. I can't. Keith's hours just got cut and I've had to start working part-time to make up the difference. We can't afford to take chances."

"On me. That's what you mean. You can't afford to take a chance on me. The girl who fails at everything."

Brenna looks distraught. We've always been close and I know she doesn't want to hurt my feelings. But it hurts that she doesn't think I can pull this off. That she thinks I'm a failure just like everyone else. She puts her arms around me.

"That's not what we're saying. We just think you should reevaluate. You were counting on a lot of press and attention from being on the show. Now that you aren't, it's going to be really hard to get people in there." Brenna speaks softly, as if the cadence of her voice can soften the blow of what she's saying.

Shame boils through my blood as I'm confronted by the evidence that no one in my family believes in me. Even worse, the fact that my father isn't here just twists the knife. My father is the one who got me into jazz in the first place. I wanted to own a jazz lounge so badly because of all the stories he told about the club his best friend owned back in the seventies.

"I shouldn't be surprised that you guys don't get it. You never really have."

Mom suddenly looks hurt. "We have always tried to support you Sasha. But what kind of family would we be if we weren't honest with you? By the time you finish fooling around, you'll have spent the best years of your life chasing foolish dreams. I don't want you to look back with regret later when you have nothing to show for it."

Her words cut me through and through. "How long have you guys been planning this little intervention?"

Brenna looks guilty, probably that she didn't warn me about what I was walking into tonight. "We just want you to find happiness. You've spent so much time working on this. You never go out anymore. How are you supposed to meet anyone if you're working all the time? I worry about you living alone. I don't know what I'd do without Evan."

I love my brother-in-law but his idea of a good time is watching sports on the couch, remote in one hand and a beer in the other. Not my thing at all.

I push back from the table. "I need to go."

There's a flurry of sound behind me as they all push their chairs back and follow me into the kitchen.

"Thanks for letting me know that you're backing out of the deal." I grab my scarf and wrap it around my neck. I motion for Brenna to hand me my coat which is hanging on a hook next to the back door.

She hands it over, watching me warily. "Why are you thanking us?"

I pull the coat on, zip it and then flip up the hood in preparation for stepping out into the chilly night air. Then I look behind me. Brenna and Audra stand by my Mom. That's kind of the way it's always been though. I've never really belonged, not even in my own family.

"I'm thanking you for letting me know early enough so that I can find other investors. Luckily I have friends who are willing to help me learn about the business side of things but I still have a lot of work to do. Including planning a grand opening on a shoestring budget."

Mom glances over at the others. "You mean you're still going through with it?"

"Just because you guys don't think it's a good idea, doesn't mean that it won't be a success. And I'm glad to know what you really think of me. I was silly enough to actually think that you guys were proud of me for trying to follow my dreams but that's only when those dreams match up with what you want me to do. I won't make that mistake again."

I step out onto the back steps, pulling the door shut behind me over their startled protests. My fists clench at my sides and I have to restrain myself from turning around and pounding on the door. But I don't have time for nonsense. It's time for me to go hunting.

I need to find twenty thousand dollars.

* * * * *

The next day, I pivot in front of the full-length mirror in my bedroom, finally satisfied with my outfit. I have to get ready to leave since Emma asked me to help her set up for the surprise engagement party she's throwing for her future brother-in-law. Despite being rich, handsome and charming, Finn is also really nice. He even got me a recurring gig at a big hotel in Virginia Beach that pays my rent most months.

When he found out that I was starting a business, he promised to introduce me to some other small business owners that can help me. More than likely, I'll be doing some networking tonight at this party so I want to look festive but professional, too. Finn knows me as a singer. Tonight, I need to show everyone that I'm a businesswoman, too.

If only I could show my own family as easily. I spent all night making plans on my ancient laptop. I can't deny that it hurts, knowing that my own family is just waiting for me to fail, but it only makes me more determined. I can do this.

I'm a businesswoman.

I repeat that to myself as I put the finishing touches on my outfit and through the entire drive to Norfolk.

Finn's penthouse is in a newly redeveloped section of the city. *A rich part of the city.* When I pull up, someone is pulling out of a space directly in front of the building. I quickly pull in and cut the engine. I look up at the impressive gray structure and have to swallow against a sudden attack of nerves. The first time I saw Finn arrive at Tank and Emma's place in a black Bentley that probably cost more than the duplex I live in, it was surreal.

Now I'm going to his penthouse.

I wonder if he has cool rich guy toys like a real life version of Batman or something. It's hard to believe that I know people with this kind of wealth. It's the kind of thing you see on television or in movies but is so far removed from your normal existence that it doesn't even register. However, it'll be different seeing it up close and personal. But this isn't just a social visit. This party has the potential to change my life.

As I gather my things, I remind myself to keep my cool when I get up there. No gawking. I need to be cool and sophisticated.

I walk into the lobby and falter when I see a guard behind a desk. Am I supposed to check in or what? Luckily before I can work myself into a state of anxiety, Emma walks in. She waves to the guy behind the desk and then holds out her arms for a hug. With her long blond hair and blue eyes, she looks so innocent. It's hard to believe that we bonded over our crappy jobs at a strip club, where I was singing and Emma used to wait tables.

"I'm so glad you're here! My sister just texted me that she's running behind so I really need the help." Emma planned this surprise engagement party for her future brother-in-law and I know she wants everything to be perfect. "Eli and Kay are still coming, right?"

"They plan to. Kay told me they were when I talked to her a few days ago."

Emma visibly relaxes. "This is going to be so much fun. Finn and Rissa are going to be so surprised!"

"Where are they anyway?"

"Tank got them dinner reservations at that new French place. They should have just arrived so we have at least two hours before they get back home."

We ride up to the penthouse and she opens the door with a key. Emma immediately puts me to work crafting crepe paper bows and hanging the small banner she had rolled up in her bag.

"So, who is this guy? The businessman?" I add when she looks at me blankly.

"Actually, I'm not sure. Finn said he knew a few people but had to check to see if they could do it. I've invited all his friends so I just assumed whoever it is will be here. Since the party is a surprise, I couldn't exactly ask Finn."

"Right. Of course."

She stops fiddling with the streamers she's unrolling. "You're really nervous about this, aren't you?"

"Well, yeah. I really need help. I just found out yesterday that my family is pulling their investment money."

Emma pouts. "Sasha, you know Tank and Finn will invest. They'd love to help."

Before she even finishes her sentence, I'm already shaking my head. "Thank you but I really want to do this on my own. The only reason I let Kay and Eli invest is because she'd badger me until I gave in. She knows all my weak spots. That's the hazard of knowing someone since grade school."

"I understand. I didn't even want to let Tank pay for my school fees so I get it. But you know we're happy to help if you change your mind."

The most amazing thing is that I truly do know. Emma doesn't have a self-serving bone in her body. She truly wants the best for everyone around her. It's what makes her such a great friend and I suspect, what makes her so perfect for Tank.

"I do know that and it means a lot. It's just that I'm so close. *I know I can do this.* But I just need to figure some things out first. I've never owned anything before. I need advice. Badly."

Emma comes over and squeezes my arm. "Don't worry. Finn mentioned that he had several people in mind so you'll have more than one to choose from. Get them drunk enough and you can ask them all the questions you want."

The intercom buzzes. Emma winks and then opens the door for the caterers.

In less than half an hour, the place looks ready to go. Most of the guests have arrived. Tank arrives finally and Emma greets him with a relieved sigh. He waves at me from across the room and then sets the case of beer he's holding on the counter.

Emma taps a spoon against her flute of champagne. "Thank you for coming everyone. Before the guests of honor arrive I just want to say—"

The front door opens and a woman with a head of curly red hair stumbles through the door backward, her arms and lips attached to Finn. The crowd grows silent and the couple freezes when they realize they aren't alone. Finn looks surprised but not guilty so I figure the woman in his arms must be his fiancée.

Emma turns to glare at Tank.

He looks down at his shoes before glancing over at Emma sheepishly. "*Oops.* I guess my guy at the restaurant forgot to call and warn me that they were on the way home."

Finn still has his hands on Rissa's behind and doesn't look as though he has any plans to move them. A giggle escapes before I can stop it. Emma still looks pissed but soon she's laughing softly too.

"Um, surprise!"

The room erupts into applause and wolf whistles. Rissa extricates herself from Finn's arms even though he doesn't look too happy about it. When her eyes light on the banner I attached to the wide living room window, she lets out a soft gasp.

"It's a party. For us!"

She grabs Finn's arm and tows him across the room to where we're standing. Even though Finn still looks murderous, Rissa grabs Emma in a big hug. "Thank you so much. I can't believe you did this for us!"

Finn shakes hands with his brother. "Yeah, thanks bro. Great timing as usual."

Tank winces and pulls his hand back. "That's what family is for, right?"

Finn kisses me lightly on the cheek. "Sasha, this is my fiancée, Rissa."

We shake hands and then she's back in Finn's arms.

"This is a gorgeous room. I love the colors." I direct my comments to Rissa. The room is decorated in mainly muted shades but with strategic pops of color. The yellow throw pillows are the kind of thing I can't ever imagine a guy buying for himself.

Her eyes light up. "I finally convinced Finn that we need a little more color in here. If he had his way everything would be beige."

Finn shrugs. "It's practical. Brown matches everything."

Rissa gazes up at him adoringly. Next to me, Emma is looking at Tank the same way. Suddenly the room feels suffocatingly small. Everywhere I go I'm surrounded by lovey-dovey types and even though I don't begrudge my friends their happiness, it's getting harder and harder not to ignore the emptiness I feel that there's no one standing by my side.

"I think I'm going to take a walk. It's a little stuffy in here."

Tank shifts uncertainly. "There are parts of this area that still aren't safe. Maybe we should go with you."

Finn eyes me knowingly. "Why don't you go up to the roof? It's got a great view and it's only accessible to residents. You can have a breather from all the noise."

I smile at him gratefully. "That sounds perfect."

After retrieving my coat, I ride the elevator up one floor. It lets me out in a small sitting area that leads to a wraparound outdoor space. Wow. I knew that Finn renovated this building when he bought it but I wasn't expecting anything like this. Most of the rooftops in the city are dirty and kind of scary looking. This looks like the outdoor seating space at a restaurant. I feel my tension start to melt away.

I lean against the brick wall and look over the rooftops of the shorter buildings in the distance. Way up here, everything looks so small. But at least I'm alone finally.

Always alone.

Until I open my eyes and see the dark shape standing next to me. Air escapes in a little gasp and I instinctively move back. The man standing there has on a long black trench coat and one of those old fashioned hats like men used to wear back in the forties. My breath freezes in my chest. It's the guy from the business office. The gorgeous one.

"*You.* What are you doing here?" I meant to say it forcefully but it comes out in such a breathy way that if I didn't know better would make me think I'm happy to see him. Which is crazy since he clearly is a stalker of some kind.

"Getting some air. I love this view."

"Of all the rooftops in all the world, huh?" I consider whether I should just turn around and go back inside. Seeing him turn up like this is seriously creeping me out.

He chuckles. "Your expression gives away everything you're thinking. I'm not some weirdo. I come up here every time I visit my brother. I'd say it's more likely that *you* are stalking *me*."

"I'm here because my friend lives in the building and recommended it. And I was here first."

He holds up his hands and backs away slightly. "Friend? Boyfriend?"

"Maybe." I'm sure he can tell I'm lying but there's no way I'm admitting to him that I'm alone.

"Lucky bastard," he mutters.

I come back to my previous spot at the wall and look back out over the city. Night comes so quickly now and the temperature has dropped enough that I can see my breath. Inhaling, I take in the cool, fresh air.

"Okay, I'll bite. Why the sigh?"

"What?"

He gives an exaggerated sigh and then bats his eyelashes. I realize that he's imitating me.

"I did *not* do that."

"Yes you did. Quite dramatically I might add. What could a girl

41

like you possibly have to be sad about?"

A little tingle of pleasure at his words is drowned out by the dismissive way he looks at me. I'm so tired of people thinking they know what I'm about. What I need.

"I'm not sad. I'm just thinking. Okay maybe I'm a little sad but only because some of the things I've been thinking about make me feel like a jerk."

"Like what?"

"I don't know why you're even asking. Clearly you don't care and we don't even know each other. We are not friends. I don't even know your name."

"Damn that's harsh. I really thought we had something. The way you looked at me yesterday. Then when you came to my house last night wearing that little black dress. I really felt a connection."

My startled laugh echoes a little. "Since that never happened I'm going to assume you've been hallucinating."

He grins and looks so unrepentant that I can't help but smile back. He really is very handsome. That little spark of recognition that I felt that first day flares again even stronger this time. I can't figure out why I feel like I know him. If we'd gone to school together, I would remember. This is not the kind of guy you could forget.

"That last part didn't actually happen? Well, you can't blame a guy for his fantasies. And my name is Gabe." He holds out his hand.

"Nice to meet you, Gabe." It feels rude to ignore him so I take his hand and shake it.

"Okay now that we're friends, why would you feel like a jerk?

You can tell me. I'm just some random guy on a rooftop. You can be honest."

I huff out a breath and scratch at a groove in the brick wall. "My friends are all coupled up and so happy. It's wonderful, really. Just not the easiest thing to witness when you're always alone."

He doesn't turn, just keeps looking over the city. The sounds of the traffic below merge with the whisper of the wind and the soft sounds of our breathing.

"It's a strange and terrible thing to be alone while surrounded by people who love you."

His softly spoken words touch something deep inside of me. I can tell that he's not just spouting platitudes or trying to make me feel better. He understands loneliness.

"Yes, it is."

We stand in companionable silence for a few more minutes before I'm aware that he's turned slightly and is now watching me.

"I can feel you staring."

When I look over at him, he's smiling. "Men look at beautiful women. Is it really so shocking?"

"I'm not going to date you. Whatever this is, it's not going to work out. Any time I'm attracted to a guy, there's a one hundred percent chance that he's a jerk. So, I'm taking a break for a while."

"So you admit that you feel it, too? Besides, I thought you had a boyfriend?" The smug grin on his face grows even wider.

Caught, I ignore the question. But just standing this close to him has already caused a number of reactions that I'm sure he's aware of.

My pulse has been racing the entire time and I'm grateful I'm wearing this big coat. I have to resist the urge to cross my arms over my suddenly sensitive breasts.

"It's okay. I'm not dating either."

I send him a dark look at that statement. I'm not sure if he's making fun of me or not but there's no way a guy who looks like him isn't out there racking up as many notches in his bedpost as possible.

"I'm serious. Finding the right person is damn near impossible and being with the wrong person, well, that's worse than being alone. Have you ever wondered if the person you're supposed to be with is right under your nose but you turned left instead of right one day and missed them?"

His question surprises me. It's way more contemplative than I would have expected from him. It reminds me that I can't assume I know anything about his life either.

"That sounds like the kind of thing that would happen to me."

At his curious stare, I find myself explaining. "Things have a tendency to go left when I want them to go right. Sometimes it feels like the more I want something, the less likely it is to happen." I start to say more but stop myself. Why am I telling him all of this?

"Why did you stop just now? What were you going to say?"

I won't meet his eyes. It feels strangely intimate, talking to him like this but I have to remind myself that he's a stranger. He's beautiful and very easy to talk to but he's still someone that I don't know well.

"It's nothing."

He makes a soft sound of disagreement. "Come on. What have you got to lose telling the truth? You don't know me and I don't know you. You can finally say all the things you really want to say but can't most of the time. All day long we censor ourselves, tone things down or edit out the unpalatable bits of life and sometimes I wonder if we're losing the ability to be honest. Everyone is so afraid of causing offense that we've ceased saying anything that really matters."

His speech feels almost like it's aimed at me. Isn't that what I do all the time? I'm constantly making decisions about what I should talk about or not talk about. There are so many things that I can't say to my parents, my sisters or even my friends because they just don't get where I'm coming from and I'd rather say nothing than argue.

"That's easy for you to say, Mr. Perfect. You've probably never failed at anything. Whereas I seem to fail at everything. My singing career. Relationships. And today I found out my family is backing out of investing in my new business. Just one more thing to add to the failure pile. I should have just stayed home tonight for a little chocolate therapy. I'm not good company right now."

He turns back to look out over the city and I'm presented again with the perfect line of his profile. The lines of stress around his eyes do nothing to diminish the beauty of his face, only emphasizing it.

"You'd be surprised by the things I've failed at. The people I've let down. I'm talking about the kind of stuff that usually results in jail time. I wasn't a very good person for a long time. But I'm trying to change."

He moves closer and tucks a stray curl back behind my fur hood. The motion forces him to lean down slightly since he's so tall and my heart rate speeds up as I catch a hint of his scent. His finger brushes gently against my cheek and my mouth falls open slightly at the soft touch. It takes all my willpower not to turn into the caress and rub my cheek against his hand.

Oh, what is it about this man? Everything about him calls out to me and makes me want to rub up against him like a kitten. The thought jolts me back to where we are. On a rooftop, in the cold, while my friends party a floor below without me.

"I should get back. The party will be over soon. I feel bad for bailing out."

"Party?" His hand lingers in the air, like he's about to touch me again. My stomach tightens, preparing for the touch, but then suddenly, he smiles.

"Yes, you should go. I have a feeling fate will throw us together again. Soon."

It seems like an odd thing to say but then again this entire conversation has been strange. So I decide not to say anything, instead giving him a small smile before I turn to go. I'm halfway to the door when he calls my name.

"Sasha?"

He pushes away from the wall and comes to stand right in front of me. In the moonlight, the masculine beauty of his face is even more apparent. He doesn't even seem real. Like he's just some illusion my mind has conjured up to torture me.

"Failing at something isn't the same thing as being a failure. That's like saying a person who falls down is the same thing as a person who can't walk. You may not have found where you belong yet but you will. And when you do, you're going to shine in all the ways that really matter."

"Thank you." His words touch me deeply. I know he's just trying to make me feel better but it still gives me a warm feeling that someone believes that I'm more than just my mistakes. That I'm destined for more.

As I ride the elevator down a floor to Finn's level, I think back on our strange conversation. It shouldn't have taken a stranger to make me see my course but when I think about it, I'd been more honest with Gabe in that short conversation than just about anyone else in my life.

And I know nothing about him other than his name.

* * * * *

A few minutes later I reenter the party. There's even more people here now and several of them look drunk already. I must have been out on the roof for longer than I realized. I fold my coat over my arm and drop it on one of the chairs facing the window. Finn and Rissa are dancing, swaying sensually in a way that says they'll be doing a lot more than dancing once they're alone again.

Maybe I should just make my excuses and go home. Even though I was hoping to make some business contacts, I really don't want to ruin Finn and Rissa's party with my dark mood. The only person who'll notice if I'm not here is Emma. I feel guilty leaving before Kay and Eli arrive but it's not like they don't know a lot of the people here. Tank works for Eli so they would have been coming anyway.

I start walking toward Emma, ready to make my excuses, when someone grabs my arm. I turn, startled to see Kay. Eli stands just behind her and nods hello.

"Hey! We just got here. Nice party, huh?" Kay looks around the crowded room.

Eli brushes a quick kiss against Kay's forehead. "Sit down and put your feet up." He whispers it but since we're standing so close I can hear him.

We both watch as he walks across the room and joins Tank, who is standing with a group of men I don't know. They clasp hands and then a few seconds later masculine laughter rings out.

"What's going on with you? You had a weird look on your face when you came in. Why'd you get here so late?" Kay asks.

Thinking of my almost kiss with Gabe up on the roof, I'm sure I did look weird when I first came in. Probably weird and sexually frustrated.

She moves to the couches set in front of the windows. I take a seat right next to her.

"Oh, I was here earlier to help Emma set up. I just went to the roof for some air. I've been distracted all day. Thinking about the club. I didn't get to tell you that I finally signed the lease for the space." I haven't told Kay about my family backing out of the deal. I know my best friend and she'll feel obligated to offer to help. I don't want her to ever feel like I'm taking advantage of her generosity.

"Congratulations! It's going to be awesome. I'm going to help and Eli has that cousin who does event planning, remember? She told me that she'd love to help you plan the grand opening." Kay leans back and sighs heavily.

She looks exhausted. She hasn't said anything yet but I strongly suspect that she's pregnant. I remember when she was carrying Hope and the main things she craved were chocolate chip cookies and afternoon naps.

"So, what were you doing up on the roof?"

I can feel myself blushing so I look around, hoping Kay doesn't notice. Finn is now behind the counter in the kitchen. There's a man sitting on one of the barstools chatting with Finn while nursing a beer.

"Do you want a drink? I'm going to get another drink. I'll be back."

"Okay, I'll just have water though." Kay looks perplexed at my sudden announcement but then Emma sits down next to her. I take the opportunity to slip away.

Finn looks up when I approach the counter and hoist myself up on one of the barstools.

"Sasha, this is my brother Zack." He gestures at the man sitting next to me. "Emma told me you're looking for some business advice. Zack is a small business owner."

So this is one of my choices. I try to check him out without being completely obvious. Zack has an impressive array of tattoos covering his arms and dark hair fashioned into a row of short spikes. He's handsome like his brothers, although in a completely different way.

"Hi. Nice to meet you."

He raises his beer in my direction. I don't know that much about Tank and Finn's situation, just what Emma has told me, but I know that they have several half siblings they never knew about. This guy is the last person here that I would have pegged to be related to Finn but when he smiles at me, there's a welcoming twinkle in his eye. Despite his intimidating exterior, I get the sense that he's a pretty easygoing guy.

I turn back to Finn. "Sorry I was gone so long. That view from the roof is amazing."

Finn nods. "I go up there all the time. It's a great place to think. Very peaceful."

I would agree but my thoughts turn to my mysterious stranger. There's nothing peaceful about the way I feel when he's around. He seems to bring out the best and the worst in me, inciting me to give a voice to my darkest desires and my most shameful truths. But he never made me feel bad about anything I revealed. He seemed to get it: how isolating it can be when you're surrounded by successful people and you know you can never measure up.

But that sense of connection was surely a fantasy. A man who looks like that could never understand what it's like to be a failure. He was just being nice.

And just that quickly I'm a little depressed again. It was nice to share that sense of camaraderie. For a little while it felt like it was just the two of us but it's time to come back to reality.

Suddenly Finn breaks into a huge smile. "Hey, you made it!"

The barstool next to me slides out and someone sits. "I was on the roof. You know I love that view."

That voice, smooth as silk, wraps around me. *Oh no.*

I turn to my left and look directly into the laughing eyes of my mystery man.

Chapter Four

Gabe

Sasha turns and our gazes collide. At Finn's introduction, she holds out her hand in greeting and I seize it before she can change her mind. Slowly, the shock in her eyes fades to be replaced by anger. After a moment she looks back and forth between Finn and I and then narrows her eyes at me.

Finn claps me on the shoulder. "Gabe is the other entrepreneur in the family. He owns the shop with Zack."

Zack leans forward. "If you have questions about the paperwork, Gabe is more your guy."

"Yeah, I'm your guy," I echo and her eyelashes flutter at the hidden innuendo in the words.

Dimly, I register that Zack is still talking but all my attention is fixed on Sasha's hand in mine, the warm silk of her skin, the fragrance that teased me up on the roof taunting me again.

She smells like candy.

My phone rings, the sound muffled through the layers of my coat. She tugs, forcing me to release her hand, which I finally do reluctantly. The sensation of her skin sliding against mine is almost worth the loss of her warmth.

She won't even look at me so I finally pull my phone out. Luke's name and number is displayed on the screen.

"Luke? Hey, I wasn't expecting to hear from you so soon." My newfound little brother has made his wishes to stay detached from the rest of us pretty clear. But considering his talents with accessing information that no one is supposed to have, I took a chance by sending him the pictures I snapped in Max's hotel room. I was counting on his sense of curiosity getting the better of him. He may not want to talk to Max but I'm sure he's wondered what the hell is going on just like the rest of us.

"I know but we need to talk. It's important."

"Were you able to get anything from the enhanced images?" The original shots were too dark and slightly blurry, probably from my haste in getting the pictures taken before I was caught. There aren't many people that I trust enough to confide in but luckily one of my best friends is a photographer. Josie was able to enhance the images enough for us to read the top part of a document in the drawer and to get an image that was on the bedside table in a frame.

"Yeah, I did. I ran the names on that letter. Can I come over?"

I glance around. I told Zack that I was involving Luke but we haven't mentioned it to anyone else. Tank and Finn have no idea and I definitely don't want it coming out in the middle of Finn's engagement party.

When I look up, Sasha's watching me and suddenly I'm regretting my candor on the roof. Is she wondering if I'm involved in something shady right now? But she's not looking at me with judgment in her eyes, merely interest. That doesn't mean I want her to know what we're talking about though. For some stupid reason I want her to see me as I am now. The man I've worked so hard to become. Something about the way she looks at me makes me want to be better.

"No, I'm not at home. I'll come to you." I glance over at Sasha again. Her fingers are wrapped around her champagne flute and as I'm looking, she crosses her legs, one shapely limb twining around the other.

"I'll come to you in a while. A long while." I hang up and put my phone back in my inner pocket.

"Problem?" Sasha raises her glass to her mouth and I can't look away. I watch every moment as her lips purse and she takes a small sip. Then she licks her lips.

Jesus.

I need to diffuse this situation carefully. I don't go after women who know my brothers or friends so that puts Sasha squarely in the off limits column. Not that she'll have a problem with that. She's made it pretty clear that she doesn't trust me and isn't impressed with my usual methods of charm and flattery.

"No. I just got something I wanted, actually. But it does mean that I need to leave a little earlier than I expected."

I'm probably imagining it but she looks a little disappointed.

"That's probably for the best." She lowers her voice. "Look, I would have never said all that stuff to you up on the roof if I'd known you were related to Finn. I'm still completely embarrassed by it all and also mad at myself that I didn't realize who you were. I knew you looked familiar but maybe if I'd spent more time around Tank lately, I would have seen the resemblance and figured it out."

"I'm glad you didn't." At her shocked look, I laugh. "You would have never told me all that stuff and I would have never confided in you either. And I needed that. I haven't felt this good in a long time. I guess confession really is good for the soul."

She doesn't look convinced. "Maybe that's true but it's still really awkward that I just told you that I'm a jealous shrew who envies her loved ones happiness and now I am going to have to see you whenever Tank or Finn has a party."

"You see, that's why I like you. I told you that I was a bad person, the kind of bad that usually results in jail time, and you actually think you're the one who has something to worry about here." I chuckle softly and finally she does too.

"I guess that's true. But you told me about stuff you used to do. Things that you've moved on from. I told you about things I'm feeling right now."

The music changes to something slow with a low, throbbing beat. I stand and shuck off my coat, leaving it draped over the barstool. I extend a hand.

Sasha raises one elegantly sculpted eyebrow. "Are you asking me to dance?"

"Yes. Just one dance."

"Why?" She honestly looks confused.

"Truly, I don't know. There are so many reasons why I should just walk away and pretend tonight never happened but you know what? I don't want to. I liked talking to you. And even if it's only tonight, I'm not ready to let it go just yet."

"You aren't?" she whispers. When I shake my head, she takes another long sip from her glass. Then she puts it back down and puts her hand in mine.

"Oh, why not?"

* * * * *

I tug her after me to the center of the floor and then pull her into my arms. She's so much shorter than I am, so the top of her head barely reaches my chin. If it weren't for the ridiculously high heels she's wearing she'd be dancing with the front of my sweater.

"So do your brothers know about, you know... what we talked about?" Sasha asks in a low voice.

She looks around us and she's so cute that I'm hit with the completely unfamiliar sensation of wanting to protect her. But from what? The thing she needs protection from most is me, especially since she already admitted that she has a tendency to fall for the wrong guys. I'm one of those guys that she needs to stay away from, the commitment phobic type – a skilled liar with questionable motives.

"They do but no one else knows. Most of that was before I hit eighteen and my juvie records are sealed. I was arrested once in college, totally not my fault by the way, but somehow the charges were dropped and the whole thing was buried. At the time, I considered it a lucky break but now I'm pretty sure that was my father's doing."

We dance in silence for a while and I have to fight to keep my hands in place. Her coat was hiding a clingy red wraparound dress that emphasizes her hourglass figure. And every time we move, her thighs slide against mine. I'm not sure why I thought dancing was a good idea. It's more like torture.

"Gabe?" She says my name experimentally, as if trying out the sound on her tongue. "You haven't gotten into any trouble lately, right?"

My initial decision to stay away from her was best. She's the kind of girl that wants to believe in the good in people. I don't want to be the one who proves to her that there is no good. There are simply those who take the opportunity to act and those who don't. But all people are just doing what is most advantageous for them.

"No, I'm done with all that. But I'll always be trouble, Sasha. It's in my nature."

"Aren't you the one who said our failures don't define us?"

I smile hearing my own words thrown back at me. She's watching me with a knowing look on her face.

"I don't consider the things I've done failure. More like character traits. Just like my hair color or eye color." The music ends and I step back. As enjoyable as it's been to be around her, I know it's time to go. There's something about talking to her that makes me forget where I am. Who I am. But I don't have that luxury right now. I need to get over to Luke's and figure out what's going on.

"Walk me out?"

She looks like she wants to protest but then she grabs her coat. I hold it out for her, watching as she slides her arms into the sleeves. I lift the heavy fall of her hair to keep it from being trapped under the collar of her coat.

Out on the street, she turns left so I follow. Finn's building is in a neighborhood in transition. It's got a great location so a lot of developers have started snapping up the buildings in the area so they can renovate them or raze them completely and create new condos. But at night, the area is still a little sketchy. There's no way I'm letting Sasha come out here to find her car by herself.

She stops next to the same steel gray monstrosity I remember. It looks even worse on second viewing as I notice all the places where the paint is peeling.

"My brother would be in pain if he saw this car. He's a mechanic. It looks like it's in dire need of medical help."

"Your brother?"

"Zack. The one upstairs with the Mohawk and all the tattoos."

"Right. I can barely keep all your brothers straight. I feel like I need a list."

"Yeah, you're not the only one."

She laughs softly and pulls her keys from her small purse. "So he's a mechanic. What about you?"

"I oversee the restoration of classic cars. It's a lot of bodywork, mostly. Zack handles repairs and we've also got a guy who deals with nothing but motorcycles."

"I can tell you enjoy what you do. I'm determined to find that for myself too. That's why I came here tonight. Oh, why did it have to be you?" Her face crumples.

I move closer and take her face between my hands. Tears pool in her eyes and I brush them away with my thumbs. "What do you mean?"

"Emma told me that Finn found me a mentor. I was so excited! Everything is falling apart and I thought this would be my chance to get some help. But now it's you. I know you don't want to help me." She crosses her arms and steps back a little. It's probably good for us to have some space right now but I immediately miss the contact.

"I think we both know that if I spend time with you, it won't have anything to do with business. I'm attracted to you, Sasha, but you're friends with my brothers. That's a line I can't cross."

She sniffles. "I know. If things got weird then we'd have to see each other. It's already going to be weird enough. But I was really counting on getting help. Now I'm not going to get the money I need

59

to open my club. I might as well just give up now."

"What's the problem exactly? You need people to invest? I invest in stuff all the time."

She narrows her eyes. "I didn't come here to beg for a handout. I already got a loan. It's just that the loan only covered a certain amount. My family was going to invest but I found out yesterday they're backing out."

My mind races, turning over the information she's given me so far. I need to stay away from her but I can help her before I go.

"Okay, so if the bank gave you a loan, they probably funded a certain amount based on items you stated in your business plan that you'd need to open. I'm going to guess instruments and speakers were a big line item."

She nods and brushes away a tear with the back of her hand. "Yeah. That's one of the biggest items on the list. They also funded me a certain amount for construction to build a stage. There were some smaller items like cleaning on there, too."

"Well, if you really have to cut costs, the easiest way is to figure out how to borrow or trade for some of those items. If you know anyone with instruments or equipment like that, maybe they'd be willing to let you borrow them. Or you could find some of the items secondhand. Then you could use the loan money allocated for instruments on something else."

She nods, her smile growing. "Or have friends who are handy help me build the stage."

"Exactly. That would be my advice. Trim costs by using

resources you already have."

Suddenly she grabs me around the waist. "Thank you!"

I stiffen in the embrace and shift, trying to keep my hard-on away from her. After one final squeeze she pulls back.

"Sorry. I was just so excited." But there's a naughty little twinkle in her eye as she says it.

"You're going to be fine, Sasha. Just fine." I brush my finger over her cheek and she closes her eyes. I take a deep breath and step back. "I'll wait for you to get in the car."

Her eyes pop open and she grins. "The only one who does that is my dad."

"Then you've been around the wrong men."

She walks around to the driver's side of the car. I wait on the curb, my hands shoved deep in my pockets to keep from reaching out for her.

Just as she opens the door, she looks over at me. "So, I guess this is goodbye then." She looks as devastated as I feel and I realize that she's feeling this same strong pull. This same sense of recognition. Not like I know her. But like I *should* know her.

Before I know what I'm doing, I round the car and pull her into my arms. My hand slides under her hair and my mouth settles on hers before she can make a sound. She recovers quickly, pushing up on her tiptoes, her lips opening under mine to accept the soft thrust of my tongue. She tastes so good and the way she's moving against me makes me think of how she'd move if I were inside her. It's madness, this pull between us. I'm not sure if it's because she's off-limits or because she's Sasha. But there's something about this girl that makes me forget myself and all my rules.

I think that I could stand here all night, enjoying the soft, wet warmth of her mouth. But she makes a soft, needy little sound in the back of her throat that accomplishes two things. It makes me hard as a rock and also reminds me where I am. On a street corner in front of my brother's building kissing one of his friends like I'm going to take her right up against the car.

I break the kiss, panting heavily. Sasha grips the collar of my coat, pulling me back down for a final, soft kiss. Our lips meet and cling before I take a step back.

"You can't just go," she whispers.

"I have to."

She looks as perplexed as I feel as she watches me back up. Everything inside of me rebels against the idea of not going after her. I've always been bold about going after what I want but in this case, that's not in either of our best interests. And my desire for her is trumped by my need to protect her.

Fine time for my conscience to show up, I think sarcastically.

"Get in the car, Sasha. Go home. It's for the best, I promise. If I come any closer, we both know what will happen. We'll burn each other up but then it'll be over just as quickly as it started. And the last thing I want to do is hurt you."

Her slender fingers tighten around the top of the car door. "I never thought I'd be saying this but I wish you weren't such a gentleman. Because getting burned up sounds really good right about now."

Her soft words make me want to reconsider my stance. The times we've spent talking have been some of the best times I've had with a woman in a long time. But between all of our friends in common and whatever the hell Luke found out about our father, there's no getting around the fact that this is not meant to be.

"It's for the best if I stay away from you, sweetheart. I promise. You've had enough bad luck."

Then with a quick nod, she slides behind the wheel. I stand on the curb and wait until she drives away.

* * * * *

As soon as Sasha's car disappears, I turn around and almost bump into Finn. "Hey, what are you doing out here? Shouldn't you be inside at the party?"

He shakes his head. "I saw you leave with Sasha. That's why I'm here. Let's walk."

I have no choice but to follow. Finn may walk with a cane but he's also an ex-Army badass who can probably take me out without ever once losing his grip on the damn thing. Once we pass his building, I realize he actually means business. More than likely he doesn't want anyone else to come out here and see him chewing my ass out.

"Let me guess, you saw us?"

He shrugs. "It's none of my business. You're both adults. But you know what is my business? When Emma is upset because her friend

63

calls crying after a one-night stand gone wrong."

"What makes you think it would be a one-night stand?"

"Because it's you, Gabe. Sasha is a friend of mine too and she's been a friend to our mother as well. It's none of my business but I'm letting you know that I'll make it my business if I have to."

There it is. I have to admire his ability to make such commonplace words sound so threatening.

"I understand."

"Good, then I should get back." He turns and walks back to the building, leaving me standing in the middle of the sidewalk. I groan and then walk back to my car.

Luke's mother owns a bakery called Anita's Place. When Finn first found out about our tangled family tree, he started coming here for a slice of pie every other day. Once I tried it, I understood why Finn kept coming back. Luke's mom is a wizard in the kitchen.

As soon as I come through the door, Luke motions to one of the waitresses.

"Hey Rory, can you bring him a beer?"

She nods and walks off. I slide into the booth across from Luke. The waitress returns with an opened bottle and places it in front of me. I nod my thanks before taking a long pull.

"You look like you needed that." Luke narrows his eyes. "Who pissed you off?"

I ignore the question in favor of getting right down to the reason I'm here. "What did you find out about those names?"

Luke glances around us then leans forward. "I couldn't find

them. I ran every variation of those names I could think of and got nothing. This is big."

"You called me here to tell me you found *nothing*? How is that helpful?" I'm not in the mood to decipher Luke's strange type of logic.

"The fact that I couldn't find anything gives us a certain type of information. The only people who can hide from me are usually pretty well connected. Like CIA government connected."

The implications of what he's saying hit me all at once. "Like spies or something?"

Luke's eyes gleam as he nods.

"Shit. What the hell is Max into? Why would he need a list of spies?" If my father has a list of these names, they're either people he knows or people he's looking for. Neither of which sounds legal at all.

"Government operatives or people in witness protection. Not sure. That's what I'm going to find out."

"But I thought you said that you couldn't find them?"

Luke gives me a smug grin. "Just because I can't find them doesn't mean I can't *find* them. I asked my online buddy Cypher to look into it. No one can hide from him. In the meantime, watch your back."

As hard as it was to turn Sasha away, this situation is the perfect example of why I need to stay away from her. Something about her draws me, intrigues me and makes me lose sight of all the logical reasons why I avoid emotional entanglements. She makes me want to do all the things I normally run from, like asking her about her childhood and listening to her talk about her dreams.

There's something about her that makes me want to share those things with her. But getting close to someone carries risks, especially since I'm not sure what kind of blowback I'll get once we figure this thing out. Whatever Max has gotten himself into, it sounds like he's in with some pretty shady people. Being involved with someone would be as good as painting a target on her back.

It's bad enough that all of my brothers have to be on guard against whatever underhanded dealings my father has in the works. But Tank and Finn are ex-military so I know they can handle themselves. Zack is street smart just like I am and I definitely don't have to worry about Luke. He's managed to erase almost all evidence of his existence online. The kid probably has several alternate identities ready to go in case things go south.

"Where were you when I called?" Luke is watching me curiously now. I realize that I've just been sitting here in a daze, not talking but just staring off into space.

Suddenly he grins. "Your mouth is all swollen. I know that look. Damn man, sorry if I interrupted you while you were busy. Or getting busy."

I laugh at his childish glee. "Get your mind out of the gutter. I was at Finn and Rissa's engagement party. I might have been … busy afterward but it's nothing serious. It can't be anything serious. She deserves better than a guy like me."

I have no doubt that Luke already knows about me. He's

probably looked into all of us. Tank already admitted that he did the same. There are few secrets amongst us now, which is for the best. I'm tired of hiding.

"But you've cleaned up. So what's the problem?" Luke asks.

"There's no problem. I just don't want her anywhere near my messy life. Whatever this shit is with Max, it can't end well. I can't drag her into this."

Luke nods and luckily lets the subject drop. As I finish my beer, a comfortable silence descends until he starts talking, hesitantly, about the software he's working on. He's been doing his best to stay away from this entire situation with Max but between my request for help and Finn's insistence on visiting him every few days, I can tell he's starting to accept that we're going to be a part of his life. And that it might not be such a bad thing.

Half an hour later as I walk out into the cool night air, my senses are on high alert. Talking about the situation with Luke has only reinvigorated my earlier fears. Max could be running from someone. Or he could be someone that others run from. The uncertainty has me looking over my shoulder. Just thinking about it gives me that creepy feeling you get from being watched.

Before I can talk myself out of it, my phone is in my hand and I'm dialing a number that I haven't used in a long time. Cole answers on the first ring.

"Wow. Gabe Marshall. It's been a long time."

His gravelly voice still sounds the same, like he's been sucking on cigarettes since birth. My relationship with Cole is complicated.

Zack hates him and blames him for teaching me how to find trouble at a young and impressionable age. But there are so many things my brother doesn't know. It's true that Cole corrupted me but in many ways he saved me, too.

"Yeah it has. I need a favor."

He chuckles. "I know what that means. Give me the info."

Cole is mainly known for boosting cars but he's also like an information network. He knows everyone who knows everyone. Anyone on the wrong side of the law operating in the southern Virginia area will be on his radar. After giving him a quick description of the scarred guy I saw outside Max's hotel, he's silent for a minute.

"I'm on it. What have you been up to kid? You looking for work?"

In Cole's world, my world, looking for work can only mean one thing. He's putting together a job and he's looking for players. For one illicit moment, I feel that old excitement, that *anticipation*. Then I ruthlessly squash it.

"Nah, I'm out of the life."

He chuckles. "No one is ever really out of the life, kid. Call me if you change your mind."

I force myself to walk to my car, ignoring the urge to check behind me again. This is the reason I decided to go straight. No more shadows around each corner. No more worries about who might be coming after me. I'm done with all that and I won't let Max's troubles drag me back in.

But as I slide behind the wheel of my car, Cole's words echo around my head.

No one is ever really out of the life.

Chapter Five

Sasha

Things have a way of looking different in the morning. So when I wake up on Saturday, I decide it's time to get proactive. Ever since my epic fail on national television, I've been in survival mode. Planning the grand opening of the club has kept my mind off of things but now that there might not be a club, it's time to stop licking my wounds and get serious. I need to find a source of funding fast.

Gabe's words come back to me. I know that he's trouble but he was right about one thing. I can't allow each failure to take me out of the game. Failing at things is a side effect of living life. Maybe singing isn't going to be my career and that hurts, but there are so many other dreams that I have. Opening this club will be a manifestation of a dream I've had ever since I was a kid.

After a quick shower, I review my schedule for the day. After the blistering safety lecture I got from Eli when he found out that I was conducting music lessons from home, I've stopped scheduling new students. Even though I know he's right, I can't help but resent the intrusion. I take a deep breath. If all goes right, I'll be scheduling new students soon in my beautiful new space.

Thoughts of business remind me of *him*. I press a hand over my suddenly racing heart, remembering that kiss. Despite his insistence on leaving me sexually frustrated, his advice last night was exactly what I needed. And even though it had been hard to hear in the moment, I actually appreciate his restraint. I don't really want to get involved with anyone right now; I'd just lost my head in the moment. What girl wouldn't with a kiss like that?

Just because I've sworn off men momentarily doesn't mean I'm dead. Gabe Marshall is exactly the type I usually fall for. Beautiful. Smug.

Trouble.

I look at myself in the mirror. "The type of trouble you don't need right now."

But damn, he was a good kisser.

Even though it's empty, I decide to spend the day at the club. There's not much I can do without fixtures but just being in the space will inspire me as I go over my massive to-do list for the opening. Plus, Gabe's advice about cutting costs makes me think. A cleaning crew is scheduled to come this week but maybe that's something I can cut. I need to go to the space and see how bad it is. Plus I just want to see it again.

There's also the added benefit of grabbing breakfast on the way. My handbag is over my arm when I hear the knock.

I pull open the door, expecting to see my landlady. She sometimes asks me to run errands for her on the weekends. But it's not Mrs. Hanes. My father is standing at the porch railing looking down to the yard.

"Daddy? What are you doing here?"

My father has only been to my place a few times. The day I moved in and to bring me some homemade soup from my mom when I wasn't feeling well. I visit my parents often enough that he doesn't need to.

He pulls me into a hug. "May I come in?"

"Of course. I'm sorry, I was just surprised." I step back so he can come in.

He shrugs out of his coat and folds it over his arm. I take it from him gently. "What brings you here so early?"

He looks around curiously, taking in the bright red color I painted on the walls a few months ago. I've always enjoyed what my dad calls a "lively" sense of style.

"I had to come. It's about the club." He takes a deep breath and then sits on the couch. He pats the cushion next to him so I put his coat down on the armchair and sit next to him.

"Dad, I know what this is about. Mom made it pretty clear that she's the one who didn't want to invest in the club anymore. I'm not angry at you."

My father has always been my biggest fan. I'm completely unashamed to be a daddy's girl. I know that my mom has tried to be supportive of my dreams but it's harder for her because she honestly doesn't understand them. Daddy has always shared my passion for music. He's the one who introduced me to jazz in the first place. When I was growing up, names like Gillespie, Coltrane and Ellington were as familiar to me as any of my relatives.

"When I figured out what they were doing, I had to get out of there before I said something I'd regret. Your mother and I argued and if there's one thing I've learned over the years, it's to avoid talking when you're angry."

I pat his hand. "This isn't your battle, Dad. I don't want you and Mom fighting over me."

He turns and looks at me for a long moment. "I never told you this but I was supposed to be a partner in the club with Tommy when it first opened."

Tommy Billings, or Uncle Tommy as I'd always known him, was my dad's best friend from high school. He features heavily in all the stories my dad tells about the old days.

"You were? I didn't know that. All this time you've talked about how much you wished you'd had your own club. What happened?"

"Charlie happened."

The story of how my father got swindled out of his life savings by a friend has practically shaped my childhood. My parents almost went bankrupt and my mother had to take on odd jobs to help them get by.

Silence settles between us and I don't attempt to break it with questions. My dad tells stories in his own time and you can't rush him along.

"When Tommy first told me he wanted to open a club, I was excited. He had a friend who was ready to go in with us. All we needed was two thousand dollars each. It doesn't sound like much now but back in those times, it was all of my savings. If things had gone wrong, I would have been bankrupt. Then my friend Charlie told me I could double my money by investing in this new company. He told me he'd done it and so had a few of our other friends."

He rubs his hands over his eyes and the sheen of tears there makes a lump form in my own throat.

"You didn't know, Dad. He was your friend. Of course you trusted him."

"I was a fool. Trusting the wrong person cost me everything."

He lets out a long breath. The sadness on his face finally gets to me so I pull him into a hug. I hate seeing my father like this, broken and ashamed. The same boiling rage I always feel when hearing this story washes over me. I can't understand how people can be so cruel. So twisted. Manipulating people who are trusting is the lowest form of crime, in my opinion. It requires that you have no conscience at all. I'd rather someone stole my things than my dreams and my faith in other people.

"Well, I know that Uncle Tommy ended up owning the club anyway. Was he mad at you for dropping out?"

"At first. He called me all kinds of stupid for losing my money to a scam but it was too late. Since I was out, he had to come up with more cash to cover my share. I'm not sure how he did it but somehow he got the money. Things were great for a while but when the club hit hard times, they had to sell it. In the end he moved on and ended up in the glass business. He's happy and has a great life but I know he wonders about what might have been just like I do. Maybe if I'd been invested with him, we could have ridden out the hard times. I don't know." He blows on his hands and rubs them briskly.

"I'm sure he doesn't blame you, Dad."

"Maybe. Maybe not. But it's something I'll always wonder about. All your mother thinks about with you girls is getting you to settle down but I don't ever want you to settle. When you get married and have a family, there are sacrifices you'll have to make. I love you girls and I love your mother. You know I do. But it is a sacrifice. Do you understand what I'm telling you, baby girl?"

He squeezes my hand and his eyes are fixed on mine. I understand then what he's trying to say. The thing he doesn't want to admit out loud. That there's a part of him that will always wonder about what could have been. That he doesn't want that to happen to me.

"I understand, Daddy. I won't settle. Never again."

His face breaks into a grin. "Ever since you were a little girl, I always knew that you were going to do things your own way. You've always been independent like that. The others take more after your mother. I love them but they don't have that same wild spirit inside like we do. They can't understand. So don't let them get you down. And definitely don't let them stop you."

"I won't. I'll just have to find other investors. Although I have to admit that I'm not quite sure how to do that."

My mind immediately goes back to Gabe and his offer to help me with the forms the day we'd met. He looks like the kind of guy who knows all about business plans and profit and loss statements. He could probably write a business plan in his sleep. Maybe I shouldn't have blown him off so easily.

I wince remembering how I'd picked him apart the first time we met. He'd been obvious but I shouldn't have ripped into him that way. I'd just been so frustrated and cranky after standing in that long line only to find out that I'd done something wrong. Again.

But it wasn't his fault he was the embodiment of the type of man that had hurt me in the past. Maybe his offer to look over my forms had been sincere. Since I'm going to be in business, I need to learn how to manage people. How to gauge who's actually sincere and who wants something from me.

Of course, it's a moot point now because all that happened before he knew who I was. Now that he knows I'm connected to Finn and Tank, he won't come anywhere near me.

"My business plan is pretty rough. If I'm going to approach other people, I need to step up my game."

He leans over. "Well you've got one investor right here."

My heart sinks. Apparently my mom didn't tell him everything that she was going to do. "Mom already said that you guys are pulling your investment completely. I guess she didn't tell you?"

He stands and retrieves his coat. "I didn't say your mother would be investing with me. I have some money tucked away for a rainy day. Your mother doesn't know all my secrets yet. And I already talked to your Uncle Tommy and he wants to invest too."

He kisses me on the forehead. "I'll see myself out."

As I watch him leave, my emotions are in a tailspin. I've gone from excited to devastated to hopeful all in the span of an hour. But overwhelmingly, I feel hopeful.

I latch on to the feeling with all I have.

* * * * *

After the impromptu visit from my father, I sit on the couch and think back over everything he told me. This new information puts a lot of the stories he's told over the years into perspective. By the time I finally leave the house, I realize so much time has passed that my craving for pancakes will have to wait. I'll have to console myself with a cheeseburger instead.

My landlady, Mrs. Hanes, is on her side of the building watering her plants. Her gray hair is wound up into a high bun and she's only wearing a light sweater despite the cool weather. I'm not sure how she can stand it because as soon as the weather changes I feel like I need to wrap myself up in several layers.

"I met your father earlier. He fixed the railing." She nods toward the slats in the railing.

Sure enough, all the slats are in place and nailed in to the banister. One of them came loose last week and was sticking out at an odd angle. I'd tried to push it back into place but I wasn't strong enough and I was scared of cutting myself on one of the nails poking out of the wood.

"Did he? Well, I'm not surprised. He worries about me."

She moves a little closer, pouring a stream of water from her can onto the potted begonia near the steps. "He had the tools in his truck. I tell you, they don't make 'em much like that anymore."

She waves as I walk down the sidewalk toward my car at the end of our drive.

Despite the cold, it's a nice day to be out. I put down the windows in my car to let in the breeze. I'm not the only one taking advantage of the last tolerable weather before winter hits hard. Several people are on bicycles and I note several mothers out pushing those jogging strollers.

I love Main Street. It's everything that New Haven has to offer in a nutshell. The picturesque businesses with their trademark red awnings overhanging the sidewalk make for a scenic walk for tourists. The side street that leads to the boardwalk is deserted but I know that it'll be busy by midday.

Even in the midst of the cool autumn weather, there are always people like me who can't stay away from the water. I moved to Virginia Beach because it was closer to a lot of the clubs where I used to perform. Plus I just wanted to get a little distance from my parents. I knew my mother would freak out if I moved too far away so I figured thirty minutes was far enough to keep her from showing up unexpectedly but close enough for her not to worry too much. Now that Kay has moved into her new house with Eli, I figured it was finally time for me to think about where I want to be.

And that's New Haven.

My new space is in a converted row house on a side street right off the main road. It's in between a vintage clothing boutique and a pastry shop. I take the first available parking space I can and then walk to the building. The sign in the window still says *For Lease*. I'll be sure to take that down after lunch.

Glancing back at my car, I decide to leave it parked where it is and just walk over to my favorite retro diner, The Rush. When I push open the door, Miss Doris looks up from behind the counter.

"Oh well, look who decided to come see me." She cackles out a laugh and comes around the counter.

I haven't seen her in a while and when she hugs me, her familiar scent of cinnamon and cigarettes washing over me, it feels so familiar. Kay and I used to come here all the time in high school.

"I just moved back in town and I've been getting settled. I'm staying over on Kent Avenue in one of those converted duplexes. I'm renting from Mrs. Hanes."

Miss Doris leads me to the counter. "Sure, I know Elaine. Her husband used to work for the gas company back when my Gerald was there. He was a nice guy. Liked the drink though," she whispers.

I can only shake my head. Now it really feels like old times. I forgot how small this town really is and how there are never really any secrets. Everybody knows your business even if you think you've been discreet. She leaves and comes back with a glass of Coke. It's a small thing but it feels good that she remembers my usual drink order.

"I'll just have a cheeseburger and an order of sweet potato fries."

She winks. 'You got it, kiddo."

I pull out my phone and start making lists. Despite having slightly less funding, I'm more determined than ever to make this club a success. Over the years I've built up an impressive list of private students but I've always done in-home tutoring. Now I'll finally have a commercial space to meet my students. One of the main reasons I was able to get a loan for this venture is because I proposed a space with dual functions. It will be a jazz club and a small theatre. And during the week when the club is closed, I can use the space for tutoring.

I was told I'd need a liquor license just to serve alcohol at my grand opening but I'm sure I'll need a different license to serve it on a permanent basis. I put that on the list. Also I'll need to figure out what suppliers to use so I can get the food and drink at more affordable prices. Miss Doris interrupts me to set my food down and I'm halfway through my burger when I finally realize that I'll have to scrap all my plans if I can't figure out how to trim expenses. I could do a scaled down opening but that's not really what I want to do. I wanted to make a splash.

I take another huge bite of my burger and console myself with the greasy delight.

On the way out, I leave cash on the table and then I stuff several bills in the tip jar up front.

I walk out of the diner and cross the street, walking down to my new building. Excitement shivers through me. It's mine! I use the key the landlord gave me to open the door and step inside. It smells musty from being closed up so I leave the front door open behind me to air things out a bit.

First thing, I take the For Lease sign out of the window and place it on the floor facedown. I'll have to give that back to the landlord later. Then I take a good, critical look around the space. When I was here before I was looking at it for its potential. Now I'm assessing its current condition. The floors are scuffed from where the previous tenants moved out and there's a thick layer of dust on everything.

In the middle of the floor are some bookcases left by the previous tenant. The landlord told me he would get them cleared out if I didn't want them but I think I'll leave them. I'm not in the position to turn down free stuff, even if I'm not sure what I'm going to do with it all yet.

There's not too much I can do until it's cleaned up in here but it's fun to dream about what it'll be like. I pull the door closed behind me and lock up.

As I cross Main Street again, I take a good look around. It's a weekend and the middle of the day and while there are a respectable number of people out shopping, it's not exactly busy. Nowhere near the kinds of traffic you'd see in Virginia Beach or Norfolk. What was I thinking to try to start a club here? Even if there are a lot of jazz enthusiasts, are there enough to support a business?

Shaking off the negative thoughts, I get behind the wheel of my car and turn the key. There's a clicking sound. I turn the key again. Nothing.

This is not happening. Come on.

Spending the day stranded in the middle of town wasn't exactly my grand plan. I have roadside assistance but the last time I used it, it took forever. I glance across the street at the diner. Miss Doris might know someone who could tow me faster. Then for some reason my thoughts go to Gabe. Didn't he say that he owned an auto shop with his brother?

No, no, no. You are not calling him.

My resolve where he's concerned is already shaky at best and there's no way that I can keep my reserve around him if we keep getting thrown together. But when I pull out my phone to find the contact information for roadside assistance, my fingers end up doing a search for Gabe Marshall. G&Z Motors is the top search result.

Maybe this is a sign. A sign that I need to go after what I want. I snort. I'm not even sure what I want, other than to figure out how to get my club open on schedule. *And to see Gabe again.* I ignore the traitorous voice of reason and before I can think about it too hard, I dial the number.

"Hi, I need to get a tow truck."

* * * * *

The man who arrives to tow my car isn't Gabe or Zack. He's a small, wiry guy who introduces himself as Jim. I climb up into the cab of the truck while he scurries around the back attaching things and then I hear the motor as my car is lifted onto the bed. Then he's back in the driver's seat and we're off.

I twist my hands in my lap, wondering what the hell I was thinking. Gabe is going to know that I'm there deliberately to see him because I could have easily called a tow truck in New Haven. My nervousness only increases as we cross the city lines into West Haven. I'm not as familiar with this part of the county but it seems a little more rustic, with lots of tall, hanging trees and lots of farmland.

Finally we pull into an asphalt parking lot in front of a shop. At the sight of the huge G&Z Motors sign hanging over the door, my pulse picks up. *Down girl.* I'm not sure why my traitorous body is reacting this way. For all I know Gabe isn't even here. I wipe my sweaty palms on my jeans. This has the potential to be really embarrassing.

"You can go inside, Miss. I'll get your car down and get it into one of the bays." Jim hooks a thumb toward the side of the building where there are what look to be several huge garage doors.

"Okay, thanks." I push open the door of the big truck and climb down carefully. The truck rumbles behind me as it pulls around the side of the building. When I push open the front door, a bell tinkles softly overhead.

Straight ahead there's a long black desk with a computer. A small stack of tires sits next to it. There's a man hunched over, typing painstakingly one key at a time.

At the sound of the bell, he looks up. "Can I help you?"

It's Zack. His tattoos are covered by the long sleeves of the blue coveralls he's wearing, but that hair is unmistakable. As I get closer, he pauses and then snaps his fingers.

"Hey, I remember you. Last night at Finn's party. You're the one Jim towed in?"

"Yeah. I'm Sasha."

He comes around the counter. "I remember. Zack."

I shake the hand he holds out and try to look around without being obvious. Would it be weird if I ask if Gabe's around? Maybe if I don't say anything I can just pay for him to fix the car and get out of here before Gabe even knows I'm here.

The bell over the door tinkles and I freeze then glance over my shoulder. A young blond guy walks in and waves at Zack. I let out a breath.

"He's not here. You can relax."

I look over at Zack innocently. "Who?"

He snorts. "I know when a woman is looking for my brother. Not sure why all the girls go for that preppy look."

At his disgruntled look, I can't help but laugh. "Well, some of us like bad boys." Despite all the tattoos and the spikes in his hair, he comes across as cute instead of scary.

His eyes twinkle. "So what happened to your car?"

"I'm not exactly sure. It just wouldn't start. It's old so I guess it's finally breathed its last. Luckily it happened after I finished lunch at least."

He smiles. "Small favors. Don't worry. We'll get you fixed up. It'll probably take a few days depending on what's wrong though."

A few days? It finally hits me that my car has just broken down. The money from my new gig has kept me current on the rent but there's no way I can afford major repairs on my car.

"Breathe. It's going to be okay." Zack takes my arm and leads me to the counter. "Let's get you logged into the system and I'll go back there and take a quick look. It might not be a big deal."

His calm, confident manner is soothing. I follow and lean against the counter, looking around while he logs onto the computer.

It's much cleaner than I was expecting. Not that I spend a lot of time in auto shops but I definitely had a different mental image. This place is wide open and modern looking. Everything is either white, black or chrome and it smells only faintly of rubber. There's a man sitting in the waiting area watching the television mounted on the wall. He coughs, a wet, rattling sound. I shudder and look back at Zack.

He hands over a form and a pen. "Fill these out and then we can get started."

After I scrawl my name, address and the make and model of my car, he takes the form back. "So, tell me. How does a nice girl like you end up mixed up with my brother?"

"That's a long story."

"I've got time. Actually, if you don't mind a little noise, why don't you come to the back and keep me company?"

"Really? I don't want to be a distraction."

He laughs. "The day I'm not distracted by a beautiful woman is the day they put me in a coffin and drop me six feet under. After the day I've had, I need a distraction." His eyes swing toward the waiting room. The man there dissolves into another coughing fit before pulling out a tissue and blowing his nose.

"Unless, of course, you'd rather wait out here."

I scurry behind the counter, ignoring his soft laughter.

Chapter Six

Gabe

When Josie called and asked to meet for lunch, I jumped at the chance to get out of the office. This morning, I'd snapped at several of my employees and a customer before Zack finally pulled me off desk duty. He put me to work in the back but even repairing a chrome bumper on this sweet 1970 Dodge Charger wasn't enough to take my mind off the prior day.

All I could see was Sasha looking up at me while we were dancing instead of the car in front of me. Instead of the wrench in my hand, my fingers kept clenching, remembering her soft skin and the way she'd fit against me when we kissed. If we ever ended up in bed together, it would be explosive and my body wasn't happy with me for denying it the pleasure.

Josie is one of the few people who understands how to navigate my strange moods. She's also one of the few people who can see through my bullshit and doesn't let me get away with anything. She'll probably get along with Sasha really well.

No, scratch that. She won't be meeting Sasha. *Because you won't be seeing her again. Off-limits.* I groan at the thought.

"What is with you today? You haven't heard a word I've said."

Josie turns in her seat and glares at me. It's probably a good thing that she's hampered by the seat belt since I know how much she hates being ignored. I always tease her about being a spoiled princess who is used to being the center of attention. She doesn't even bother to deny it anymore.

Most people see the two of us and assume that we're together but it's never been like that between us. I'm the first to admit that it's weird that we've never been anything but friends. Josephine Harlow is a certified bombshell. With her pale skin, long wavy dark hair and plump lips, she looks like a pinup girl. But there's no chemistry between us. When I see her I just see Josie. Not soft skin and kissable lips. Big doe eyes and …

"Gabe!" Josie is watching me closely and now she's smiling. "Seriously, what is going on? I haven't seen you like this in … well, ever."

"Sorry. I've been distracted."

"I was telling you about my new exhibit. You keep spacing out.

You're being even more of a dick than usual." Suddenly she stops smiling. "Does this have anything to do with those pictures you asked me to work on?"

Josie has been incredibly curious about the pictures and I feel paranoid but I refused to talk about it over the phone. After hearing what Luke discovered, my suspicions don't seem so far-fetched. My father has documents relating to what could possibly be top-secret government spies. Which means that he's either totally innocent or totally evil. Because I can't think of too many reasons for him to have those names in his possession.

"Strangely enough, no. Not that I'm not worried about that though. I am. I'm not sure if I should say anything to Max about it. But I'm starting to understand why Luke is so determined to stay away from him."

"Do you really think your father is into something illegal?" She shoots a worried glance at me.

"I don't know. But I have to find out. Someone was watching me that day at the hotel and if that's the case, how do I know they aren't still following me? Or Zack? Or our moms? Where does it end? I have to figure out what's going on or I'll never feel safe."

"So what are you going to do?"

I pull up in front of the shop and cut the engine. "I don't know but I promised Zack to help him with a rebuild this afternoon so we'll have to figure it out later."

I get out, surprised when she follows me to the door. "You're coming in?"

"Yeah, sure. I'm not ready to go home yet. My mother's been on my case lately since she found out about the new exhibit. I can't take it anymore."

Josie's photography career has long been a point of contention with her upper crust parents. They'd much prefer that she'd gone to law school like her older brother. Instead she's been doing portraits and when they found out she's participating in an exhibit showcasing eroticism in art, they've been coming down on her harder than usual.

"You're welcome to crash at the house tonight if you want. You know we've got plenty of space."

She grins. "That would annoy Zack and that's always a bonus but I've got a date tonight. I do need to pick up one of my sweaters that I left at your house, though."

Chuckling I push open the door to the shop. The waiting room is empty but I can hear the sound of voices from the back. Then laughter.

"It sounds like Zack is in a good mood. That's a shock." Josie follows me behind the counter and into the office.

As soon as I turn the corner, I stop in the doorway. Sasha and Zack both look over at me.

"Sasha? What are you doing here?"

My initial shock morphs into pleasure at seeing her again. Sasha smiles back at me shyly. Her eyes reflect back the same feelings I've been struggling with all morning. Desire, longing and then the strangest of all, joy. Last night I'd resolved that I wouldn't pursue her so in my mind that was the end of it. But seeing her like this, out of the blue, I can't deny that it makes me feel happy.

Josie appears at my elbow. Sasha glances over at her and her expression closes up.

"My car broke down. Zack said I need a new battery and a bunch of other stuff that I didn't understand."

"Your car is in good hands. He's so much nicer to cars than he is to people." Josie smirks at Zack.

His fingers tighten around the pen he's holding. I'm not sure why Josie loves to annoy him so much but it's been going on since high school. I've given up on ever figuring out their weirdly antagonistic relationship.

"Actually, I haven't found that to be true at all. Zack was just giving me some advice about my new business venture, actually. I had no idea he was a musician, too." Sasha grins at Zack affectionately.

The sight sends a sharp stab of envy straight through me. When I look over at Zack, he's watching me closely. So I work to keep the scowl off my face. By his smirk, I'm not successful. My brother loves screwing with me.

"Zack, Josie needs to pick up something at the house. Would you mind giving her a ride? I have some paperwork I need to finish up before I can leave." If nothing else, it'll get him away from Sasha so I don't feel this insane urge to reach over and drag her away from him.

He nods and then chucks Sasha under the chin. "Hang in there, Maestro."

I grit my teeth against another shocking spear of jealousy at seeing that casual touch. Josie and Zack leave so I walk over and sit in the chair behind the desk. Sasha watches me and then clasps her hands in her lap.

"So ... Zack is really nice."

"You said that already."

Sasha smiles knowingly. "No, I didn't. How come you're here with me and not going back to the house with your girlfriend?"

"Josie has never been my girlfriend. Why are you here? No auto shops in New Haven?"

She looks away and the tops of her cheeks color slightly. I instantly feel like an asshole.

"Sorry. I shouldn't have said that."

"You were just pointing out the obvious. That I'm stupid for coming here. I wasn't going to and then I just found myself looking up the number for your shop."

Her words bring a smile to my face. She's been thinking about me too. The pissy mood I've been in all day seems like a distant memory.

"I'm glad you did. I haven't been able to stop thinking about you since last night. I shouldn't have kissed you but I'm not sorry I did it."

"Neither am I. But I'm still stupid for coming here. I doubt I'm your type." Her eyes skitter away from mine and one hand comes up to play with the ends of her hair.

"I don't have a type." I'm not sure if she's trying to make a reference to skin color or not but I definitely can't let her leave thinking that has anything to do with why I'm keeping my distance.

"I've dated women of every background."

She laughs. "Of course you have. What am I thinking? I'm sure your ex-girlfriends could all compete in the Miss Universe pageant too. You probably have one from every country. Like stamp collecting."

Now that makes me laugh. She has such a snarky sense of humor. In a way she reminds me of Zack. That's probably why they seem to be getting along so well.

She stands and grabs her coat from the back of her chair. "Look Gabe, we both have our reasons for not wanting to get involved. I'm not sure what I was thinking by coming here. I just wanted ... " She stops talking and suddenly looks down at her hands.

"It's okay. I know."

And strangely enough, I do. She was struggling with the same thing I am. The same thing that had me tossing and turning in my bed all night imagining her under me. I've never considered myself that creative but last night my brain conjured up a hundred alternate endings to the night, each one culminating with me and Sasha in bed together.

"Gabriel!"

At the shrill call, all amorous thoughts leave my mind. I stand and rush to the open doorway. If I have any chance at all of keeping Sasha on the outskirts of my life, I need to head Paula off before she sees her. I skid to a stop in the doorway right before she enters the office.

"Hey, are you looking for Zack? He went back to the house

already."

Paula regards me with shrewd eyes. She tries to look around my shoulder but I lean against the doorframe, effectively blocking her.

"I know. He's the one who told me you were here. I was coming to invite you and your friend for dinner at our house."

I groan under my breath. If Zack told her I have a girl here, there's no stopping her. Paula is relentless when on the hunt for information. I move back and allow her to push past into the office. As soon as Paula sees her, her eyes swing back to mine. She's practically beaming.

I am going to kill my brother.

"Sasha, this is Paula. Paula, this is Sasha Whitman. She's friends with Finn and Tank."

"It's so nice to meet you. Zack told me that you were stranded here. If you're stranded, you might as well stay for dinner."

My eyes close and I have to take a deep breath. This is going too far. Zack has no idea how he's tormenting me. He thinks it's funny but he wouldn't laugh if he knew how hard I was struggling to keep my hands off this girl. I'm pretty sure our new relationship with our brothers won't withstand what will happen if I get involved with Sasha and things go sour.

"She's not stranded, Mom. I was going to take her home." I'll take her home and then that'll be the end of it. Now that I know she's friends with Finn, I can be prepared to avoid her in the future.

"This is your mom? It's so nice to meet you, Mrs. Marshall."

Paula guffaws. "Oh, I'm not Mrs. Marshall. I never was. Neither was Gabe's momma. Neither of us wanted that bastard's name."

Sasha's mouth falls open. Her lips open and close several times before she finally says, "Oh. You're not Gabe's mom? I'm sorry, I must have heard wrong."

"I'm one of his moms. Technically I'm Zack's mom but I might as well be Gabe's as well. Now you come along and tell me all about how you met my boy."

Paula hooks her arm through Sasha's and she has no choice but to move with her or get yanked off her feet. She looks back at me for help and I just shrug. She's already on board the train to crazy town and there's no getting off now.

She's about to see firsthand just how screwed up my family is.

* * * * *

When I was in high school, I had something I called the asshole test. Meeting new people always came easily to me but keeping friends was a bit more difficult. But the first time I invited someone to the house was my litmus test for whether we'd be friends or enemies.

It wasn't easy being the kid with two moms before that kind of thing was done. Zack and I always knew our home life wasn't typical. The way Paula tells it, she and my mom were best friends until they found out they were dating the same guy. Then they were enemies until they realized they were both pregnant. They decided to ditch the guy and keep the friendship. They've raised us together ever since.

I sit across the table from Sasha and watch as her head volleys back and forth between Paula and Debbie. Ever since Paula dragged her out of the shop, she hasn't said much. I'm not sure whether she's appalled or just in shock from information overload. My family can be a lot to handle even for me on some occasions. Surprisingly, Sasha seems to be handling it really well. When I introduced her to my mom, Debbie, she offered to help her with dinner. The three women seem to have bonded over organic cooking while they were in there.

"Would you like another helping of quinoa, Sasha? It's a new recipe I got from the man at the store. He was so helpful." Debbie holds up the bowl and at Sasha's nod, plops another spoonful on her plate.

"He's probably trying to get a date. They always hit on her when we're grocery shopping. It's like I'm not even there," Paula laments. Sasha giggles and looks over at me.

"Actually he did ask me on a date. We're going out next Friday." Debbie holds up her hand and Paula gives her a high five.

Sasha's fork hangs in midair and I can tell the moment she figures it out. "Oh, you're not … "

"They're not together," I finish. "Most people make that assumption. They never have been."

Debbie laughs. "I have to give it to you honey, you've handled things better than most of the birdies they bring around. Our situation is unusual and it tends to bring out the worst in people."

"So Gabe's other girlfriends were rude? That's awful." Sasha looks over at me as if it's my fault.

"Gabe doesn't bring girls home. Zack hasn't for a while. But I remember back when they were in high school, there were some kids who teased them a lot. Called us names. I'm sure you can imagine. Then when people would see us out with a man, they decided we were immoral harlots running some kind of prostitution ring out of the house."

"I'm sorry."

Paula shrugs. "West Haven has gotten a lot better but I remember how things were about twenty years ago. This is a small community and some people can be closed-minded. But we weren't going to let them run us off. This is our home. My family has lived in this part of Virginia for ten generations."

"You're actually the first girl Gabe has introduced to us." Zack shovels another bite of mashed potatoes in his mouth and smirks at me.

I'm going to kick him in the shins as soon as I get the chance.

"Really?" Sasha looks over at me in shock. "Well, Gabe has been nice enough to help me out with some business questions."

Paula glances over at me. "*Is that right?*"

My mom doesn't seem to have picked up on the undercurrents of the conversation yet and I can only hope to get Sasha out of here before she has both of them interrogating her.

"That's right. Sasha is a singer and she's opening up a jazz lounge soon."

My mom pipes up, "You know Paula once dated a bass player in a jazz band."

I let out a breath but when I look up next Paula is still watching me.

*　*　*　*　*

Sasha gives both Debbie and Paula a hug, then waves to Zack. "Thanks for dinner. I had fun."

"We did too, honey. I'm sure we'll be seeing you again."

Sasha doesn't reply to that. I follow her out and we walk silently down the path leading from the house to the driveway. She looks over at me finally, a mischievous look on her face.

"I'm glad I stayed tonight. I thought about making up some excuse and going home but I would have missed out by not getting to meet your family. They're awesome."

"Yeah, they are. I guess you understand now why I said I've never cared what anyone thinks. I learned at a young age that it doesn't matter. All that matters is what I know."

"And you were lucky to learn that so early." She glances behind us at the house. "They are super proud of you. I can see it in the way they look at you. The way they talk about you. My dad has always been proud of me and I'm lucky to have that. But I wish my mom and my sisters didn't think of me as such a screwup."

"I know I'm lucky to have them. I wonder sometimes what my life would be like if Paula hadn't come up with the plan for them to stick together. If she'd taken Zack and raised him on her own. I might have known that I had a half-brother but I probably wouldn't have seen him often. He'd be as much of a stranger to me as Tank,

Finn and Luke are. Which would suck."

"Yeah. I guess I didn't really think until now how messed up it is that you guys didn't know each other before."

We've reached my car and we both pause. I can tell she doesn't want to end the evening any more than I do. I look up at the stars. Out here, away from all the lights in the center of the city, it's so easy to see them. It's one of the main reasons I chose to stay in West Haven. I can't imagine living somewhere that I can't see the stars.

I look over at Sasha and she has her face turned up to the sky as well. The bright lights are reflected in her eyes and she looks like she's glowing. I lean down and our eyes meet. Then I place my lips on hers. Her mouth softens under mine, accepting, savoring. It's a sweet, simple kiss, nothing like the hot, passionate, claw-your-clothes-off kiss she laid on me the night of the engagement party. That kiss was about desire. This kiss is about longing. It would take an army to stop me from taking the sweet comfort she's offering.

When I lift my head, we're both panting. I rest my forehead against hers while I catch my breath.

"I guess you have to take me home now." She folds her arms across her body, like she's preparing for a blow.

"I wish I didn't. But you are way too good for me."

She laughs softly. "You confuse me so much. I've never felt chemistry like this with anyone. Maybe that's what makes this so difficult. That thing, whatever it is, every time I see you it hits me right between the eyes. I know you feel it, too."

I blow out a breath, searching for the best way to tell her my story. She'll never understand what I meant when I said she was too good for me until I tell her.

"I used to be a thief."

Startled, she drops her arms. "A thief? Like you used to stick up people in the streets and take their wallets?"

Even in the middle of a serious moment, Sasha can make me laugh. "Nothing so obvious." I chuckle, relieved to see her smile again. "Or so violent."

"Oh, now I get it." She makes a face. "When you said thief it threw me off but I already figured things out at the party, Gabe. You told me you could have gone to jail and since you own an auto garage, it seems obvious. You used to be a car thief." She doesn't seem particularly concerned about it.

"I did steal cars. Among other things. I could have gone to jail."

Sasha nudges me with her arm. "People make mistakes. Sometimes they change their ways and get better. I mean, look at you. I'm not saying it was right but this doesn't change how I see you, Gabe. You were a misguided kid but you weren't out there hurting people."

I clamp down the unexpected swell of emotion her words bring. Her understanding wasn't what I was expecting. Most people, even those who are openminded, usually show a little hint of disdain when they find out about my past. Even though she doesn't know the full extent of the things I've done, her words give me hope. Maybe she could one day truly accept me, all of me, including the less than honest urges I still struggle with every day.

"It's only sheer luck and the intervention of people who cared about me that saved me. Without them my life would look very different right now." I stick my hands in my pockets to keep from reaching out and tugging on the stray curls flying around her face in the wind.

She tilts her head. "Well, that's pretty depressing. What I was going to say doesn't sound nearly so bad now, so thanks for that."

I can't help but laugh at that. "I guess it is."

"I used to have so many dreams. I always thought I'd get a recording contract, fall in love and travel the world. But so far my plans aren't working out so well and I can't talk about it with my family because they don't understand why I can't live life the way they do. My sisters want to fix me up with their friends or men from church and I know why they're doing it. They think that I'll marry one of those guys and then I'll suddenly want the same things they do: a white picket fence and a ring on my finger. They just don't get it and I don't know how to explain it to them."

The last part comes out as a whisper.

"What do you want?" She's watching me with those big beautiful eyes and suddenly it seems vital that I know the answer to that question.

"*I want to live*. I want to be challenged. And I don't want to settle. Ever again. But I guess the joke's on me since I haven't achieved any of the things I thought I would."

She suddenly looks over at me and lets out a little nervous laugh. "I'm sorry. You've had to worry about things like going to jail and

I'm over here lamenting all the family and friends who are so worried about me."

"You have every right to want to live your life your way."

She looks up to the sky. "Maybe I should give up on all these impossible dreams and marry a nice guy with a good job and benefits. But just the thought of that makes me feel like I'm dying inside. I don't know what's wrong with me."

"I do." Her eyes swing to mine and I open the driver's side door before I finish. "You, Sasha Whitman, *are bored.*"

I get behind the wheel and wait until she scrambles around the car and climbs into the passenger seat. I put the car in gear and start backing down the drive while she struggles to fasten her seat belt.

"That's not what I am. I have a very exciting life. I have great friends. I go out and party sometimes. I teach my music students and I perform. My life is not boring."

I pull out onto the main road. She's still staring at me from her side of the car and I can feel it.

"Don't be mad. I'm not trying to insult your life. I'm sure there are many interesting things around you but they're all things you've been doing for years. And maybe that's okay for some areas of your life but a woman like you, no, you can't settle when it comes to your personal life."

She finally relaxes against the seat. "No, I can't. Not anymore."

"I've seen you in action and I've seen that fire inside you. You want excitement. You want adventure. You want to wake up every day and wonder what new and glorious thing is going to happen.

You want passion and until you get it, you'll be bored. I should know. I'm bored, too. But we're going to fix that."

"We are? How?" She looks over at me with interest.

"By being friends." I grin at her and then gun the engine.

Chapter Seven

Sasha

This is a business meeting, not a date. I repeat the words to myself as I prepare to meet Gabe for lunch two days later.

I hold up a basic black dress and then switch arms to hold up a maroon sheath adorned with festive gold designs. My love of texture and willingness to experiment with color is one of the mainstays of my personal style. But I'm trying to turn over a new leaf and be a businesswoman so I might have to tone things down a little.

After Gabe drove me home Saturday night, he came back the next day to return my car, Zack following him in his Audi. Before they left, he told me to plan for lunch on Monday so we could go over my budget.

Apparently he's decided that since we're friends now that he's going to help me with my business plan. *This is a business meeting.* I know that I should just tell him that I'll find another mentor. I'm only torturing myself by continuing to lust after a guy that I know isn't the staying kind. But I can't help it. There's something that draws me to him and I can't seem to cut that invisible tie.

I hold up the black dress again and make a face at the mirror. It works but it's so plain. I don't want Gabe to see me like that even if it's not a date. Then I remember that I was planning to do some cleaning today. I can't be too cute because I have work to do. I settle on a satin blouse in different shades of rose paired with my favorite jeans.

He suggested meeting at one of the nicer restaurants in town but I asked to meet at The Rush. Not only because I feel more comfortable keeping things casual but also because it's so close to the club. After our meeting, I have to go wait for my first furniture delivery.

Luckily Gabe didn't seem to care about the change. I remember the way he looked at me that night under the stars. The things he told me about his past. He didn't have to do any of that. I think he really does want to help me.

Which he can't do if I'm not prepared.

I focus on the task at hand. Most of my paperwork and notes for the business are in this big, purple file folder I've been using to compile everything. But I can't show up to a business meeting with that. Gabe would probably laugh in my face.

I transfer everything into a plain manila folder and then fasten the notes together with a binder clip. If I'd had more time, I would have typed up all my handwritten scribblings. But I'll just have to make do.

I don't have time to think about it anymore because my cell phone reminder goes off, which tells me that I'm about to be late. I step into my favorite pair of four-inch nude heels and then grab the manila folder. I tuck the folder, my notes and my phone into an oversized tote bag and head out the door.

Just as I open my car door, my eyes stop on something across the street. There's a guy walking toward me on the opposite side. He's wearing a leather jacket and a ball cap pulled low over his eyes but despite his relaxed pace, he doesn't seem to be out for a friendly stroll. He's not doing anything but something about the way he's walking sets my instincts ringing. He looks tense, like he's walking with a purpose but trying to look like he's wandering aimlessly. It's how I imagine it would look when someone was casing a place before they come back to rob it.

After all those safety lectures from Eli, I'm probably paranoid. There are definitely benefits to being someone he considers a friend, such as the amazing security system he installed here that I couldn't have afforded on my own. But he tends to view everyone as a potential criminal and clearly his warped viewpoint has started to rub off on me. This poor guy is just taking a stroll, minding his own business and I've got him pegged as a felony in progress.

This is a pretty safe neighborhood but still, it doesn't hurt to be mindful. I climb into the front seat of my car and watch his progress behind me in the rearview mirror. Once he's out of sight, I start the car and back out of the driveway carefully.

The entire drive over, I mentally review what I plan to accomplish today. If Gabe can review my operating budget, then at least I'll know if I'm on the right track. Then I can move to the second stage of my plan today which is to start tackling some of the items on my action list. Cleaning is the number one thing on the list I can do without help.

I park in front of The Rush, looking around at the other cars in the parking lot. Maybe this wasn't the most professional place to meet but at least if Gabe reviews my plans and tells me they suck I can get a chocolate shake to console myself.

Inside, I grab a booth in the back. Miss Doris isn't on shift today so I give my drink order to Patsy, a middle-aged mother of two who also works over at the library part-time. How do I know all of that? Because she tells me in between explaining the specials and asking what all "that stuff" is for when I pull out my file folder.

I can't help but laugh as she walks away. It's going to take a little while to readjust to small town life.

Gabe enters the diner and when he spots me, heads to the back. Today he's wearing casual clothes again, jeans and a long-sleeved Henley shirt under a leather jacket. No glasses. No hat. Just Gabe. It's nice to see him like this with all the layers stripped off.

"Nice place. I like the fifties thing they've got going on in here."

He slides into the booth across from me, his long legs bumping mine beneath the table.

"This place is an icon. I used to come here with my friends in high school a lot. It's been here for years."

I pick up my folder, busying myself in looking through the papers inside so he won't see how flustered I am. Gabe has agreed to help me but he's made it pretty clear that friends is all we'll ever be. I have to stop blushing and stammering like a schoolgirl around him or he's going to change his mind about helping me. If I'm ever going to prove to everyone that I can do this, I need his help.

Gabe peers at me. "Are you okay? You have dark circles under your eyes. You look exhausted."

I have to laugh. Honesty seems to be the thing that binds us together. "Is that your line today? I thought you were supposed to be charming?"

"Charm doesn't work on you. You cured me of trying that the first day we met. You'll always get the truth from me." He smirks and sits back in the booth.

I roll my eyes and hand him the two-page document. "Here's the budget I drew up."

Based on Eli's advice, I used online software to create the budget. The first page is the overview with a small graph and the second page contains detail on all the expenses.

"How did you come up with these numbers?" Gabe flips the page and looks at the detailed list of expenditures.

"Some of them are just rough estimates. But for the things like cleaning and construction, I got quotes from local businesses on how much they would charge for those services."

"Good. It's best to get as close as possible on the expenses. I can't tell you how many times I've been blindsided on how much things cost running the shop. How much contingency have you built in?"

We're interrupted when Patsy brings two glasses of water and my iced tea. "Hi, what can I get you to drink handsome?"

Gabe gives her that blinding smile and I can practically see her melting next to the table.

"Water is fine for now. But I'll have a cheeseburger and fries. Sasha?"

"I'll have the same. And a chocolate shake, too."

As soon as she leaves, I take a long drink from my iced tea. Gabe watches in amusement as I drain almost half of it away.

"Are you okay?"

I push the glass back. "No, I'm not okay. What is a contingency? And how was I supposed to know to get one?"

I'm in the middle of what feels like a full-scale panic attack when Gabe puts his hand over mine. Immediately I stop breathing.

"Relax. You've already done the number one thing any business owner can do if they aren't sure about something."

"What's that?"

He leans over and says, "Ask for help."

His calm, rational demeanor makes the panic recede. My hand flexes slightly under his and when I turn my hand over, our palms meet. That has my pulse increasing for another reason altogether.

He leans back and the cool air against my exposed palm reminds me where we are. I look around but luckily no one noticed my little freak out session.

"So, what is a contingency?"

Gabe points a finger at the bottom of the budget. "It's usually the last line item under expenses. It's basically just a number that you estimate for emergencies. A cushion. Let's say that the cleaning you've budgeted at three hundred dollars actually ends up costing you five hundred dollars."

"I'd be two hundred dollars over budget, right?"

His eyes glow in approval. "Exactly. But if you have a one thousand dollar contingency, then your bottom line would still be okay. You'd actually be eight hundred dollars in the black."

Patsy appears then with our food, so I push the files to the side of the booth. Then she reappears a few minutes later with my chocolate shake. Gabe glances at me and then takes a bite of his burger.

"Chocolate therapy already?"

I pause with the straw halfway to my mouth. "How did you know about that?"

"You told me, remember?" His eyes twinkle with laughter as he takes another bite of his burger.

Mentally thinking back to all the things we talked about on the rooftop that night, I shake my head. "You remember that? I have to watch what I say around you."

"Paying attention to people is one of the things I do best. And you should definitely watch what you say around me. I have a long history of using the things I learn about people against them."

His reference to his past makes me wonder. Just who is he trying to warn off? Me or himself?

* * * * *

After we finish our burgers, Gabe takes out a pen and starts putting check marks next to the items he thinks I can trim. His suggestions line up with the same things I've been thinking. Cleaning, instruments and construction are the main areas where I think I have some wiggle room.

"Most construction estimates are heavy on the labor costs. But if you can find someone willing to help for a lower rate, then you'd have your stage built for a fraction of the cost and you could use the money budgeted for that elsewhere."

When Patsy appears with the check, she lingers for a few minutes making small talk while clearing our dishes. Her gaze is all over Gabe and she's asking him so many questions. Where he's from, what he's doing in New Haven. If he's my boyfriend.

I choke on the last sip of my chocolate shake. "Um, no he's not … we're not."

Gabe rescues me. "We're friends." He winks at her. "And now we're friends too, Patsy."

Patsy gives him a saucy smile. "I could use a few friends like you." Then she sashays off with her tray balanced on her shoulder, an extra swing in her step.

Even though I understand why getting involved with Gabe is a bad idea, it still sucks to watch other women flirt with him. *Imagine how much worse it would be if you were dating.* Gabe is the kind of guy who attracts women without even trying and a lot of those women wouldn't care if he was taken or not.

What if he hadn't been such a gentleman the night we met? I'm not fooling myself that he'd have fallen instantly in love with me. Chances are pretty good that the same thing would have happened with Gabe that happened with all my other relationships. I would have gotten attached and he would have left.

Same story, different ending. Except I'd be sitting across from him hurt and angry while watching him flirt with another woman right in front of me.

Mentally rolling my eyes, I pull out my wallet to pay for our meals. Before I can even open it, Gabe drops several twenties on the table.

"What are you doing?" I hold up my wallet. "This was a business meeting so I should pay."

He ignores me and pulls on his leather jacket. Whistling, he makes a show of looking around as though he can't hear anything.

Despite my attempts to be annoyed, a laugh finally escapes. "Gabe, I'm serious. You're doing me a favor so I should pay."

He makes a face. "Okay, that's never happening. And the second most-important rule of business is, if someone is trying to give you money, *let them*."

Shaking my head, I stand when he does and slip into my coat. He gathers all the papers that we've been looking over and slides them back into the manila folder. He's taking this business mentor thing really seriously. I'm sure he's got plenty of other things he should have been doing today but instead he's here helping me.

It's kind of sweet.

"So, where is this little club going to be?" Gabe walks beside me out to the parking lot.

I pause next to my car, suddenly self-conscious about how rough it looks. Car payments eat up a lot of money and I learned early that if I wanted to survive as a starving artist, nice cars were out of the question. My eye is immediately drawn to Gabe's sleek, black Audi on the far end of the lot. I don't know much about cars but I'm sure it's expensive. My old clunker may not look like much but it's paid for. And that makes it very attractive to me. And whatever Zack did to it has it running like new.

"It's right across the street from here." I point to the buildings directly across. "This part of town has some of the oldest buildings in New Haven. Those used to be row houses and then they were converted to commercial spaces about twenty years ago. The landlord has been struggling to keep it leased since the economy went south. It was even rumored to be haunted at one point. I plan to use that in my promotional materials. Maybe I'll do a Halloween special next year and see if I can get some local theatre groups to perform."

"That's smart. See, now you're thinking like a business owner. I told you it wouldn't take long."

His praise feels good but even better is the way he's looking at me. Like he's proud of the progress I've made so far. I stuff that feeling down deep. I shouldn't have this giggly, euphoric feeling just because Gabe thinks I'm smart. Even though no one else has ever made me feel smart before.

"You're going to show it to me, right?" Gabe starts walking across the parking lot. I have to scramble to keep up. The heels I'm wearing are perfect for a business meeting but not for running.

"Wait, Gabe. What are you doing?"

He nods across the street. "I want to see where your club is going to be. After looking over the budget and listening to you talk about what it means to you, I'm invested in the outcome now. Plus, it's in a haunted old building."

His enthusiasm is catching. After looking both ways, we cross the street together. Gabe takes my hand once we reach the other side. "Where to?"

I point straight ahead and have to resist the urge to yank my hand back. What is it with this guy and the mixed signals? He's the one who said that we can't be more than friends but then he's holding my hand, telling me I'm smart and just making me like him.

I'm so deep in my thoughts that we actually pass the doorway. "Wait, it's right here."

My keys are of course at the bottom of my bag. Gabe is staring at something behind me. I turn and look over my shoulder. There's someone getting out of a car on the other side of the street and a woman holding a dress bag entering the store next door.

"Sasha, I don't mean to alarm you but we need to get inside. Right now."

My hands finally close around my keys. "Okay, here's the key right here."

He plucks the key ring from my hand and unlocks the door. It swings open and he pulls me inside with him. Then he shuts the door and flips the deadbolt.

"Gabe, what are you doing?"

He grabs me by the hand and pulls me further into the building. "I'm hiding."

Exasperated, I yank my hand back after he pulls me behind one of the bookshelves still sitting in the middle of the floor. "Yes, I can see that. But who are we supposed to be hiding from?"

Gabe leans down to peer between the shelves so I do, too. Where we're standing we have a clear view of the front window. "Him. We're hiding from him."

Just then a guy with dark hair strolls casually past. I hate stereotyping people but everything about this guy makes me want to take a step back. His dark hair is gelled down and he's wearing a worn black leather jacket. But it's not the clothes. It's his expression. Cold. Like anyone in his way had better move because he'll have no problem taking them out. He looks completely out of place in this neighborhood.

Just before he's out of sight, he turns his head to look directly through the front window. A shiver runs through me. At that angle, the dead look in his eyes is clear but worse is the thin scar that cuts across his cheek bisecting his face.

Gabe looks like trouble. This guy looks like he should be

carrying around a body bag in the trunk of his car. He also looks vaguely familiar.

"Friend of yours?" I whisper.

"Not exactly."

"Okay. So why are you hiding from Scarface?"

Gabe looks grim. "Because this isn't the first time I've seen him. Would you excuse me for a moment?"

He moves away slightly and pulls out his cell phone. I take the opportunity to look around the space. I pull out my file folder and dig until I find the sketch provided by the general contractor who'd given me an estimate on constructing the stage. He'd decided that we could use the back right corner without impeding the flow of movement in the rest of the space.

It's so hard to imagine how different it's all going to look in just six weeks.

"Sasha?"

I look up to see that Gabe has ended his call. But he looks agitated. "Is everything okay?"

"Yeah. I just need to go check on something. Are you going to be okay by yourself?"

"Of course. I'm going to be here alone a lot over the coming weeks. There's so much to do. The first shipment of furniture should be here this afternoon. Then I can get started putting things in place."

I drop my tote bag next to the back door and open the blinds to let in the light. "There's so much I want to do here. I just hope I can do it justice."

Gabe comes to stand next to me and peers out the window. There's another set of row houses behind our block separated by a small garden pavilion. There's several benches arranged in a semicircle.

"I can easily see myself going outside to eat lunch some days or taking a break to relax before going home at the end of a long day. I can see myself here and that excites and scares me."

"Scares you?"

I shrug. "Because if this doesn't work out, I won't just be losing the club. This is something I see more as a purpose. Something my life sorely needs right now. I just want to feel like something I do matters."

I turn and he's looking down at me with an expression of wonder on his face.

"You're important to so many people, Sasha. How can you not know that? Your family, your friends, hell even Finn threatened to castrate me if I screwed around with you."

My mouth drops open. *"Finn said that?"*

A slow grin eases over his mouth. I love that expression on him. He's so serious most of the time that it's a joy to see when his guard drops.

"Not in those words exactly. It was a little more subtle, something about not wanting to have to make our business his business. It loses something in the translation. I think you had to be there to see the menacing look in his eyes."

A warm feeling flows through me. "So that's why you said we

117

have to be just friends?" It makes me feel a little better to know that he wasn't lying about that.

"That actually happened after you left. But I knew all along that my brothers wouldn't be pleased if they saw us together. Tank and Finn both consider you family now. I heard about how you've been visiting their mom along with Emma."

I shrug, even though it makes me sad to think about it. "Emma lost her parents so she's really attached to Claire now. I was happy to go with her. Everyone needs a little laughter and girl talk sometimes."

"Maybe that's what draws me to you," he whispers. He's talking so softly I'm not sure he even means for me to hear him. "I couldn't figure out what it was that kept drawing me back to you. Kept me thinking about you even when we were apart. But it's that kindness. That sweetness. You're just so *real*. It makes me want that for myself."

His hand slips underneath my hair, his thumb tracing a drugging path back and forth behind my ear. I have to clench my stomach against a wave of longing. Everything about Gabe Marshall turns me on and I don't think he even realizes it.

"Gabe…"

That's all I get out before his mouth is on mine. We back up and I jump when my back hits the wall. I stretch up on my tiptoes and anchor my arms behind his head. Every time he touches me it's the same, this sudden scorching blaze that seems to tear through all my resistance. His other hand comes up to frame my face.

He's such a contradiction when he holds me like this, like I'm precious and like he wants to take me on the floor at the same time.

His hands move to my waist and his fingers inch down, down, down between my legs. I pant against his mouth as he rubs me through the fabric of my jeans. I look up and he's watching me. I nod my permission and he slides the zipper down.

The sound in the quiet space is the most erotic thing I've ever heard. He holds my gaze as his hand slips beneath the waistband. Then I can't keep my eyes open anymore because he's stroking me, gentle little flicks across the lips of my sex, like he's just teasing me.

"I'm supposed to stay away from you. I'm not supposed to be here. But I just can't help myself." His words sound almost angry but then he takes my mouth again as one finger slides deep.

I break apart, crying out his name, the soft sound echoing around us in the quiet of the room. He stays with me, thrusting gently, letting me ride his finger. When I open my eyes he's watching me intently.

"That was beautiful. *God damn*." The hand on my cheek tightens, holding me still so that I can't avoid his eyes. What I see there shocks me.

He looks … hungry.

When he slides his finger free, I want to cry out again at the loss. I can see him closing up right in front of me, putting his desire back behind whatever wall he uses to keep himself so remote. It's heartbreaking to witness after seeing him so open just a few minutes ago.

He kisses me on the forehead. Part of me wants to drag him back down for a real kiss but I can sense that he's working through something. And I can't force him to want the same things I do.

"I have to go. I would stay and help but I need to check on something."

"You should be careful. If you want me to think you're a bad guy, you have to stop being so nice."

Gabe gives me a crooked smile. "It's all an illusion. Lock up behind me."

"Okay, I will. Trust me, I've gotten the safety lecture from Eli a million times."

He runs his hands over his hair, taming the strands that I set in disarray while I straighten my clothes. Then he follows me to the front of the building. At the door he pauses, taking one last look at me before he steps over the threshold. He waits, watching until I turn the lock on the door. Then with one final salute, he's gone.

As soon as he's out of sight, I sag against the door. My blood pressure is still high and if I close my eyes I can still feel his fingers, his lips, his tongue. To Gabe, fooling around is just a little fun and games but for me, it's just one more thing that pulls me in closer. Makes me forget myself. The man is dangerous and I don't have time for dangerous.

I shake my head. "Enough daydreaming. It's time to get to work."

* * * * *

Every weekend, my sisters and I used to attack our house with cleaning rags in hand. It was understood that chores had to be done before we could go outside and play or, once we were older, go out with our friends. Brenna used to complain every single time and even Audra would try to convince Mom that we could save chores for Sunday after church. Neither approach ever worked but it didn't stop them from trying.

Strange as it sounds, I kind of enjoy cleaning. It's one of the few things you can do in life and see instant results. So saving a few bucks by cleaning the building myself seemed like a no brainer at the time.

Before I got started.

I've mopped the floor, cleaned the bathroom and figured I'd give myself a break from chemical fumes by cleaning the thick layer of dust off the bookcases with a damp rag. I'm just getting started when there's a knock at the door. I peel off the rubber gloves I'm wearing as I approach the front door. But when I see who it is, I drop them on the floor and pull the door open with a squeal.

"Uncle Tommy!"

"Hey kid. Your Dad told me what you're doing." He pulls me into a hug and then looks around the space. "You're really doing it, huh? I had to come by and see it. I hope you don't mind."

"Of course not! Come on in." I step back and allow him inside. He pulls off his cap and walks to the middle of the floor.

"This is a great space." He points to the small counter on the left side where the previous tenant had a small coffee bar. "It looks like it's already got a lot of what you need."

"Yeah I'm going to use it for concessions."

His eyes shine as he turns in a circle. "I can't wait to see what you come up with." He looks at the rags and cleaning supplies I've left in a pile on the floor. "But I can see you're busy. I'll get out of the way."

"I'm so glad you came by. Dad told me you're interested in investing in this place so once I work out the details, I'll let you know. I really want it to feel like the original club. My dad is really excited about this."

"I am, too. You can't even imagine." He gives me another hug.

Once I get the stage built and everything is clean, I'll have to make sure he and my dad come down to help me set up. It'll be fun for them to work on it together, the way they would have before if things had been different.

After Uncle Tommy leaves, I pick up my gloves and rag. I stand, fighting another wave of exhaustion. I should have just stuck with the cleaning service. I think I remember Finn mentioning that his fiancée owns a cleaning agency. Maybe I should have just asked for a friendly discount instead of trying to tackle all this on my own.

Another sneeze catches me off guard and leaves a burning pain in my chest and throat. I pause with a hand over my chest. The pain settles after a minute but leaves a lingering ache of exhaustion all through my body.

I move back a little and my foot catches on an uneven floorboard. "Whoa!" My legs buckle and I go down hard on my bottom. The rag I was holding lands with a wet smack next to me. I roll over slightly, moving off the uneven section of the floor. I lean closer to look at the uneven wood and then groan. This place is starting to feel cursed.

If someone falls in here, they could sue me. I'm sure it's the landlord's responsibility to fix the floors but how long will that take? And if I have to wait for the floors to be redone then all the furniture that's just been delivered will have to be moved.

I sway as a strong wave of dizziness comes over me. The floor spins beneath my feet as I sit back down and rest my head on my knees. The pain in my chest is back and it's starting to feel like my throat is burning.

I'll just wait until this passes, I think. But I must have inhaled more of those cleaning fumes than I thought because as soon as I close my eyes, I feel myself falling.

Chapter Eight

Gabe

"Gabriel. I wasn't expecting you today."

It's something of a shock to see my father answering the door of his own suite. He's using a cane and looking pretty proud of himself. I know he hates to use his wheelchair but the sight of him without it makes me nervous. As conflicted as my feelings are toward Max, I don't want anything to happen to him.

"I called. I know I usually come on Wednesdays but something came up. I need to talk to you."

"Of course. Come in. I was just catching up on some correspondence." He steps back so I can enter the suite. It's quiet today. Usually he has Carol or any number of other attendants hovering over him.

"Where is everyone?"

Max grunts. "I fired them all. A man can't even walk on his own two feet without everyone causing a ruckus."

Suddenly I understand. Carol must have tried to tell him to use the wheelchair again. "You know, you can't just keep firing your staff. One day they're going to believe you and not come back."

Max sinks down into the couch and then rests the cane next to him. There are a few pages of stationery and a pen on the table next to him. He picks them up.

"Somehow I don't think you came here to talk about the way I treat my staff."

"No, I didn't."

He waits patiently for me to get my thoughts together, writing something on the paper while I'm trying to figure out how to approach him.

In all the time I've been coming to visit, I've never asked him directly why he did what he did. Maybe because I didn't think he'd tell me or maybe because I didn't really want to know. Tank and Finn have both said that he refuses to discuss it anyway. But it's time for me to put my personal feelings aside. The guy following me is clearly connected to my father somehow since he's only shown up since Max came to town.

"Someone followed me today. A man I've seen hanging around here before. Is it one of your guys?"

Max suddenly looks more alert. "Followed? Are you sure?"

"No, I'm not sure." That's the most frustrating part. I can't be sure if I'm taking this out of context or assuming the guy must be following me just because I've seen him multiple times. "But I've seen this guy more than once. He has a scar that's hard to miss."

Max's hand jerks and the pen leaves a dark trail across the paper. "Scarred? On his face?"

"Yeah. It's on his cheek." I put my finger at my cheekbone.

He's positively white now and his hand is shaking so hard that I reach over and remove the pen and paper he's holding. At my touch, he seems to come back to himself. "I apologize, I need to cut this short."

I look down at my watch in surprise. The terms of Max's financial agreement with each of us requires that we participate in hour-long visits each week. For whatever reason, he's determined to spend time with us and always seems genuinely happy when I show up. He's never cut a meeting short before or missed one except for when he was hospitalized.

He knows something. One mention of the scarred guy and suddenly he looks like he's seen a ghost?

"Whatever you've gotten into, maybe we could help if we knew what was going on."

Max shakes his head. "No one can help. But I'll take care of this. Don't worry about that man. He won't bother you again."

"You don't know that. Clearly he wants something or he wouldn't have been trailing me today. I asked around about him. A guy like that sticks out in a small town. He's been seen coming out of the old meat packing plant on South Trade Street. Maybe I should go ask him what this is about."

When I stand, Max turns pale and shakes his head violently. *"Stay away from Blade."*

This is the first bit of information he's let slip. It doesn't escape my notice that he must be pretty rattled to make that kind of mistake.

"Who's Blade?"

"Someone I'd hoped you'd never meet."

Max looks pained. It's the first time he's looked guilty and it doesn't make me feel any better. His hand lands on the head of his cane, rubbing over the smooth metal surface as if to calm himself down.

"I'll take care of this, Gabriel. In the meantime, stay away from him. His business is with me but there are people in this world who will hurt those closest to you just to make a point."

I think about Sasha, alone in her building. That guy was following me but what if he comes back there when she's by herself? What if he hurts her because he thinks she has information about me?

"What do you know about him? Tell me!" I want to shake him, force the information out of him. He must see the intent in my eyes because he shrinks back into the couch.

The door leading to the hallway opens. The men who enter are familiar. Max's security team is always nearby.

"Everything all right, Mr. Marshall?"

Max doesn't look at me again. "I'm more tired today than usual. I need to rest. I'll see you next week, Gabriel."

Dismissed, I turn and leave the suite. I need to get to Sasha.

* * * * *

I break a multitude of laws as I navigate through the early evening traffic. It's not quite five o'clock but clearly most of the city of Norfolk has gotten off work early so they can get in my way. I dial Sasha's number. It rings several times and then goes to voicemail.

"Come on, Sasha. Pick up." I dial her number again but this time I leave a message asking her to call me.

I cut over a lane and take a side street, then gun the engine. I know enough shortcuts to get me to the interstate faster but when I finally pull out onto I-64 West, I curse at the line of cars ahead of me.

This is going to take forever.

I glance at the clock on the dashboard. This nagging feeling that something isn't right is getting stronger by the minute. There's a chance that Tank is already in New Haven so I could call him. Ask him to check on Sasha for me. Even as I have the thought, I decide to save that as a last resort. Tank is extremely protective and he considers Sasha a friend just because Emma does. I know my brothers don't judge me but that doesn't mean they want their friends getting involved with a guy like me.

The traffic inches along until I finally pass an accident on the side of the road. After that the traffic opens up and I fly over the road and take the exit for New Haven.

The street where Sasha's future club is located seems much more isolated now. When I was here earlier, in the brightest part of the afternoon, it didn't look sinister at all. But it's getting dark earlier and earlier now that we're getting closer to winter. I park and look around at all the shadows between the buildings. There are too many places where someone could hide. Sasha will be leaving the club at night and anyone could be waiting out here, hidden from view.

I don't like it all.

I knock on the door and wait. I know she's here because her car is still parked in front of The Rush. There's no sound inside and I don't see anything through the glass. I bang on the door again and then turn the door handle, satisfied when it holds fast. At least she's kept the door locked.

But where the hell is she?

I peer through the glass again. Several of the bookshelves look like they've been moved and there are some boxes in the corner that I don't remember being there before. That must be the delivery she was waiting on.

Then I see it. *There.* A small lump on the floor. I wouldn't have even noticed it if it hadn't moved.

"Oh no. Sasha?"

I glance behind me, left and right. There's no one around so I dash back to my car and pop the trunk. I reach into the small black bag in the trunk and pull out my torque wrench and pick. Hopefully no one will come around the corner in the next few minutes or I'm going to end up having to explain to the cops why I keep lock-picking tools in my trunk.

I doubt they'll buy the excuse that it's a just-in-case kind of thing, even though it's true.

Kneeling in front of the door, I insert the torque wrench into the lower part of the keyhole. Since I used Sasha's key to open the door earlier, I already know that the cylinder turns clockwise. I turn the wrench to the right and then insert the pick and press up gently. I feel my way until I find the one pin that doesn't move like the others. I push that one up with a little more force and then set the others. Then I turn the wrench all the way to the right and the door opens with a soft click.

Just like riding a bike, I think.

Sasha is sitting up now, staring at me. The light coming in from the open door spills across her, illuminating the room. "Gabe, what are you doing?"

I slip the pick and wrench into the inner pocket of my jacket and kneel next to her on the floor. There's dust all over her face and in her hair. "I saw you passed out on the floor."

"How did you get in here?"

I extend my hand and help her stand. She sways against me. When she buries her face against my shoulder, the heat coming from her skin shocks me. I put a hand to her forehead. Her skin is burning up.

"Sasha, we need to get you to a doctor. You're sick."

A soft sigh escapes. "Did you pick the lock on the door? I saw you but I couldn't tell what you were doing."

Shit. I'd hoped she was too out of it to see that part. But I'll never lie to her. "Yes, I did. I told you I'm a very bad influence."

"Can you teach me to do that?" She grins up at me but her eyes are slightly unfocused. She doesn't look good at all.

"No, I'm not going to teach you how to do illegal things. Come on. I'm taking you to the hospital."

"Okay, okay but that sounds way more boring than learning to pick a lock."

* * * * *

Sasha refuses to go to the hospital but agrees to go to the clinic at a pharmacy near her house. I roam the store while she's seen by the nurse practitioner on call. Twenty minutes later she comes out looking miserable.

"It's just a bad cold so they can't give me anything for it."

"Well, then I'll have to give you my own personal remedy for colds. Wait here."

She sits in one of the plastic chairs in the waiting room at the pharmacy while I dash around the store collecting items.

Ten minutes later we're leaving with over-the-counter cold medicine, a carton of orange juice, a small jar of honey and the magazine I didn't get to finish reading.

Sasha gives me directions to her house but by the time I pull up in her driveway, she's asleep. She doesn't even stir when I stop the car. It's obvious she's exhausted and not just because of her crazy cleaning spree today. The dark shadows under her eyes were there even at the party on Friday night.

What drives her so hard?

Guilt creeps in. I could see that she was exhausted this afternoon at lunch but I still mauled her as soon as I got her alone. Instead of giving in to my libido, I should have stayed and helped her. My advice to trim expenses was never intended to be used as a reason for her to exhaust herself by trying to clean that entire space alone. Add on top of that the fact that she's obviously been sick and still thinks she can do it all by herself. I have to wonder about her life that she's so determined to prove herself that she won't accept help even when she obviously needs it.

I touch her arm and her eyelashes flutter against her cheek. "Gabe? Where are we?"

"Home. Come on, let's get you inside." I come around to her side of the car and she leans on me heavily as we walk up to the house. It's a nice place, a duplex. The windows on the right side are lit up. "Your neighbor must be home."

"Mrs. Hanes. My landlady. She had the house converted to a duplex after her husband died so she could rent out the other side. I don't want her to see you."

"Are you ashamed of me?"

Even sick, she manages to give me a quelling look. "This is a small town. The last thing I want is everyone gossiping about who I have coming and going."

"I'll make sure to sneak out later if that makes you feel better, okay?"

She smiles and pulls out her keys. Once we're in, I look around her place curiously. Most of the outfits I've seen her in have been eye-catching. Bright colors and figure hugging. It doesn't surprise me to find that her place looks the same. Her vibrant spirit invades every corner of the house from the bright red paint color on the walls to the colorful Aztec print rugs on the wood floor. I can tell the home is older but it's been well taken care of.

"Okay, I'm here. I'm going to take some of that cold medicine and go to bed. You've done your good deed for the day so you can go." Sasha's words dissolve into a coughing fit that ends with a wet, hacking sound. Just listening to her is painful.

"Not a chance. Come on."

When she doesn't move, I pick her up and start walking. She swats at my shoulder weakly.

"If this is how you sweep a girl off her feet, your technique needs work." Her head falls against my shoulder as if she's too tired to hold it upright anymore.

"Dammit, stop trying to be so strong and just let me take care of you." The first room off the hall is mainly empty except for the bed so I figure that's a guest room. I continue to the next room and push the door open with my foot. Angling my shoulders, I turn so I can fit us through the doorway without bumping Sasha's head.

Now this really looks like her. The bed is covered with a ruffly purple comforter and there's a mountain of pillows covering the bed. I set her down gently and ease her back. She sighs deeply and then turns her face into her pillow.

"I'll be back with your medicine in just a second."

Before I can leave, her hand reaches out and snags my sleeve. "You really don't have to stay. I can call someone."

"Okay, who are you going to call? Your friend Kay?"

Her eyes don't meet mine. "You aren't planning to call anyone, are you? Well, I'm not leaving you here alone."

"I can't call Kay," she whispers miserably. "She'd come running but she has a fiancé, a baby and a bun in the oven. She loves me and would do anything for me but I can't do that to her."

"What about your sisters?" I know that if anything ever happened to me, Zack would be right there.

"I could call them." She makes a face and pulls the comforter over her legs.

"But you don't want to."

"So they can say I told you so? They think I can't handle this. They think I should stick to being cute on stage, not trying to be the one in charge. I don't need to hear that right now."

Even sick and exhausted, she's determined to be strong. If her sisters think she can't handle owning a business, I have to wonder if they're spending time with the same person I am.

She shoves the pillows aside until she can get into a comfortable position.

"Well, you know what that means. Until you're strong enough to kick me out, I'm here. Now sleep."

"Thanks, Gabe." She tucks the covers under her chin and smiles up at me sweetly before her lashes drift down.

There's an unfamiliar feeling in my chest as I look down at her, something I'm not sure I'm ready to examine yet. "I'll just move my car to the street and then go get your medicine."

And then I make my escape.

Chapter Nine

Gabe

I wake to the sound of retching. A cough. Then another choked sound of agony. Sasha's guest bedroom is right next to hers and I crashed in here after calling Zack to let him know I wouldn't be coming home.

I rub my eyes with my hands and glance over at the clock on the nightstand. It's a little after two in the morning. I climb out of bed and then walk down to the kitchen. I've got a pretty good immune system but I've had enough hangovers to know what helps when you've been vomiting. I fill a glass of water and then open the pantry. There's a box of crackers on the top shelf so I grab that. She won't be able to handle anything heavy right now.

In Sasha's room, the only light is coming from the bathroom. "Sasha? I brought you some water."

She pokes her head around the doorframe. "You're still here?" Despite how exhausted she looks, her eyes light up when she sees me.

"I told you I wasn't leaving. I'm here until you can kick me out. Are you okay?"

"Fine. I just coughed so hard that it made me throw up. Which was both painful and gross."

"Here, this should help." I hand over the water and she accepts it, wrapping both hands around the glass. "I've also got some crackers if your stomach is upset."

I wait while she takes a sip of water and then walks back to bed. She puts the glass down on her nightstand and then crawls back under the covers. I don't want to leave her alone just yet so I crawl onto the other side of the bed, on top of the comforter, then open the box in my arms and hand her a cracker. She laughs softly.

"You're pretty good at this." She looks up at me curiously before taking a small bite of cracker. "I know you said we're friends and all but I have friends I've known for years who wouldn't have stuck around for this."

The way she's looking at me makes me a little uncomfortable. Like I'm some kind of savior. No way in hell I can live up to that.

"It's not a big deal. Anyone would have done the same."

"They really wouldn't have. Believe me, I know. There's no way I can see my last boyfriend measuring out my medicine and bringing me crackers when I'm nauseated."

Hearing her talk about the bastard she was dating, the one who had the right to slip beneath these blankets and curl up with her, makes me want to hit something.

"He sounds like an ass. I might not be your boyfriend but that doesn't mean I don't care about what happens to you. I like you, Sasha."

She wrinkles her brow. "I don't think I've ever had a guy say he likes me. He might like how I *look*."

"I'd be a liar if I said I didn't like how you look. You're beautiful. But you're also smart and vibrant and fun."

"Most people would probably say I'm too silly. I've always had my head in the clouds and I know that gets on some people's nerves." She shrugs but her lashes come down to shade her eyes. I can see the characterization bothers her.

It bothers *me* that the people around her consider her bubbly personality something to be ashamed of. When she looks at me, it's like she sees who I am and not what I've done. Even when she caught me picking the locks at the club, she didn't look at me like a criminal or assume the worst. Remembering her request for me to teach her to do it too makes me smile.

She's one of the few people in my life that can make me laugh and makes me look for the extraordinary in the everyday.

With a gentle finger beneath her chin, I tip her face up so she can't hide from me. "There's nothing wrong with being a dreamer. You hope for the best and try to find joy wherever you are. You make me look at the world differently. And I like how I feel when I'm around you."

After a few moments, her eyes leave mine and she reaches for another cracker. "I like how I feel around you, too."

Over the next two days, Sasha gets better. When she finds out her parents are coming to check on her, I use the time to pick up some clothes but other than that, we stay holed up in our own little universe. In between her naps, she asks me about growing up with Zack and about my relationship with my father. I ask her about the violin in her closet and then tease her about the vibrator buried in the back drawer of the nightstand. We eat takeout and watch movies, most of which she falls asleep on.

Mostly I watch *her*. Whether she's sleeping or eating or laughing or crying, everything about her fascinates me. I've never had so much fun doing nothing.

"Wouldn't it be great if we could just stay in this little bubble, just you and me?" Sasha sighs as the credits roll on the movie we just finished watching.

During the film, she snuggled up closer and closer until she ended up with her head pillowed on my chest and one of her legs twisted around mine. I have no idea how the film ended because fighting an erection for the past hour took all my concentration.

"Maybe if we don't move, we can just stay like this forever. In our pajamas eating takeout and no one will bother us."

I know exactly what she means. The past few days have been a dream in a way. Away from my usual routine, my family, my job, I've been able to ignore the voice in the back of my head that warns me I'm playing with fire.

"That's not the way it is, beautiful. The outside always comes crashing in at some point." I'm saying the words for her benefit and my own. Because when it's just the two of us, it's easy to forget why I shouldn't be here. It's so easy to fall into the fantasy that I'm the kind of guy that deserves this life.

"But could we pretend? Just for a little while." Sasha looks up at me, her nose brushing against my cheek. Longing, sharp and sweet, makes me squeeze her a little tighter. Looking down at her I have to face up to an uncomfortable truth. I'm not here because Sasha needs me anymore. The first two days she was ill but she got over her cold once she got some sleep. She's not sick and hasn't been for a while. I'm here because there's nowhere else I'd rather be.

I'm here because walking away from her is harder and harder every time.

She seems to sense where my thoughts are because her lashes lower. "Don't say it. Please. Just let me have this moment before we have to go back to reality."

She shifts and her hand lands on my chest to steady herself. My heart is banging beneath my ribs and when she feels it, her eyes lift to mine again. Whatever she sees there seems to make her brave because her hand slips down to the waistband of my sweatpants. Then she cups me through the soft cotton.

"Fuck!" I can't hold back at the jolt of pure pleasure that races up my spine.

Sasha is just as bold as I would have expected because she's got me in a firm grip, the kind that means business. Her brown eyes are heated as she swipes her thumb up and down the length of my cock, biting her lip when my fingers tighten around her waist.

"You're playing a very dangerous game, beautiful. Because my self-control is pretty much nonexistent when it comes to you already."

She slides one leg over my lap, straddling me. "Good. I don't want you controlled. I don't want your lines or that phony face you show to the world. I want you. The real you."

* * * * *

Sasha's lips crash down on mine, hot and sweet and I have to grab the back of her nightshirt to keep my hands from going crazy. I want to touch every inch of her, stroke every bit of her smooth skin until she's panting beneath me. But I know that I need to have slightly more finesse than that.

She tears her mouth from mine finally, taking several deep gasping breaths. Already her eyes are slumberous, her cheeks flushed with her desire. An intensely masculine sense of satisfaction makes me grasp her tighter. I put that look on her face. I made her lose her breath.

And I'm the one who's going to have her screaming under me.

Sasha pulls her nightshirt over her head and then squeals when I stand suddenly, holding her securely against my chest. Her arms tighten around my neck in a stranglehold and her legs wrap around my waist. It brings her right up against my dick in a way that she can't avoid.

"Oh!" She glances down and then back up at me, bashfully.

"That's right, beautiful. Get used to feeling him because he's always ready around you."

"Well, I understand that. After all, I feel the same way. I want you, Gabe." She nuzzles her nose against my cheek and does this little arch thing with her back. It rubs her right against me in a way that almost makes me come right then and there.

"Fuck, baby. You are killing me here." Blindly, I turn toward her bedroom, not even looking where I'm going, just determined to get her horizontal. Her hands tighten in my hair and she pulls my mouth back to hers, sucking my tongue into her mouth.

I almost stub my toe as I stumble through the doorway into her room and it's nothing more than blind luck that lands us on the bed when I finally collapse. Sasha drops her arms over her head, suddenly demure. Then she arches her hips. Without a word I understand her signal and hook my fingers into the sides of her panties and her pajama bottoms. Her eyes don't leave mine as I slide them down.

Her breathing speeds up as they hit the floor but she keeps her legs squeezed together.

"Open up for me, baby." My voice sounds heavier than usual, raspy but damn if I'm not already on the edge of insanity. I want to go slow, savor her and bring her more pleasure than she's ever known but there's a fierce need to dominate and possess riding me. A need to splay her open and sink in, to take her fast and hard until I'm so deep she'll never even think another man's name.

"Gabe, you can't look at it." Her cheeks color pink and the contrast against her gorgeous brown skin tone is insanely arousing.

"I'm going to be doing a lot more than looking at it, beautiful." I gently nudge between her legs and then notch her legs over my shoulders. "I'm going to be looking and touching and tasting."

She lets out a little huff that morphs into a low moan at the first brush of my tongue against her pussy. Her mouth falls open and she lets out the sexiest little whimper that hits me right between the eyes.

I work slowly, knowing that every soft brush of my tongue will push her higher, make her crave what I can give her. I trail my fingers up and down her legs. She's so soft. Everywhere. I can't get enough of her taste, drawing her little clit between my lips over and over.

"Gabe!" Suddenly her back arches and her legs tighten around my head.

It's a heady feeling, having her pliant and trusting beneath me like this. I want to get inside her in every way. I smile against her thigh, taking a little nip that makes her moan before giving her what she wants.

When I take her clit beneath my teeth gently and thrust a finger inside, she lets out another soft cry and shudders beneath me. I want to lap it all up, every bit of her desire, and then do it all again.

She's still panting when pull back and yank my shirt over my head. Kicking out of my sweatpants, I lower myself on top of her. Her hands immediately grip my hair, pulling me to her for another deep kiss.

Making my way down her body, I skim my tongue over the tempting curves of her breasts, stopping to take a nipple deep. Her helpless sigh eggs me on and I tongue the sharp peak until she gasps and squirms beneath me. I feel drugged, the scent rising from her skin so enticing that I have the urge to rub myself against her until it's all over me.

"Gabe, don't stop." She shudders when I move to the other side, treating her other nipple to the same teasing caress.

"I'm not stopping, beautiful. I couldn't even if I tried." I flex my hips and my cock nudges against her core. She gives an appreciative murmur and swivels her hips in response.

"Jesus. You're a sexy little thing, you know that? You love to tease."

She bites her lips and nods, her breath coming a little harder when I flex again.

"Well, you're not the only one who can tease. I'm not giving you this until you beg me for it."

Sasha's eyes light up and then her legs wrap around my waist. Her undulations rub her right against my dick. Fuck. She's so hot and wet. I hang my head, trying in vain to get control of myself. I groan when she kisses her way up my neck and then takes my lobe between her teeth.

"I'm not the one who'll be begging," she whispers. Then her hands drop down until she grabs my ass and holds me against her.

Control gone, I almost come right then. "Please tell me you have a condom."

She points to her nightstand. I lean over and yank the top drawer out. There's a strip of three in the back of the drawer. Rolling one on should give me the time I need to pull back from the edge but then Sasha rolls over and touches me tentatively. My cock jumps in her hand and she glances up with a naughty look before she licks the tip. Fire races over every inch of my skin as she sweeps her hair over her shoulder and opens wider, trying to take in more. When I bump the back of her throat, I almost black out when she swallows around me.

"Fuck it, you win." I pull back and get the condom on in record time. Then I crawl over her, pulling her legs around my waist. Before she can say anything, I thrust deep.

Her head falls back and she lets out a long, agonized moan. Her pussy clenches around me, holding me tight.

"*Oh my god*, I'm pretty sure we're both winning right now."

The laugh takes me by surprise and I have to smother it against her neck. Only Sasha could make me laugh at a moment like this. A sudden rush of affection takes me off guard. She has such a pure heart. I shouldn't be here, reveling in her sweetness. I'm more aware in that moment of how utterly unworthy I am of her. My heart is black, covered in years of grime from all the questionable choices I've made in my life.

But here in this moment, she makes me feel brand new.

"You don't even know what you do to me." My words are spoken so softly that I doubt she hears me but her arms tighten around my shoulders.

Before long, we have a perfect rhythm and as my hips roll against hers, I swear I'm getting deeper every time. She grasps at my forearms helplessly, her eyes widening when I hit a certain spot.

"Gabe! Yes, right there." She comes with a sharp cry and her nails dig into my skin until I'm sure she's drawn blood. Her pussy flutters and the strong contractions pull me over the edge, too. I groan against her hair and squeeze her tighter, feeling like I've died and come back to life simultaneously.

We stay like that, breathing hard and wrapped up in each other's arms for a long time. She traces circles on my shoulder and rubs one of her legs up and down mine. Those little touches seem almost as intimate as what we just did. It's like she doesn't want to be separated from me yet.

When I turn my head, she's watching me but there's no regret in her gaze. She looks completely satisfied. Replete.

Every masculine instinct I have roars to life at having put that look on her face. It may be wrong but I'm going to take this stolen moment in time and enjoy it. I can't be what she deserves but I can give her this. I will worship at the altar of her body and give her the one thing I can.

Pleasure.

* * * * *

Thursday morning I cram my feet in the flimsy pair of flip-flops that Sasha keeps near the door. When I went home, I just grabbed a pair of sweatpants, clean underwear and a few shirts. I didn't think about footwear. I really need to keep a gym bag with sneakers and a change of clothes in my car from now on. Not that I'm planning on more sleepovers in the future but just in case.

Just in case she gets sick again? Yeah, right.

I'm shamelessly taking advantage of the situation to spend time with her but even I know it's unlikely that Sasha will ever need my help like this again.

When I got up this morning, I spent a long time just staring at Sasha. I'd intended to get up after she fell asleep last night and go back to the guest room. I've never particularly liked sleeping next to someone. You end up getting too hot and fighting for the blankets. But I fell asleep with her ensconced in the cradle of my arms and woke up feeling warm. In more ways than one. I haven't slept this well in a long time and I can't even begin to examine what that means.

I open the front door, trash bag in hand, and then stop at the sight of a black SUV in the driveway. Sasha seems pretty concerned about her neighbors seeing a man at her place, which seems really old-fashioned to me. But I don't want her getting shit about me being here so I turn around to go back in when the guy calls out my name. He slams the door and walks up the driveway.

"Eli? I didn't recognize you at first."

I've met him a few times at Tank's place before seeing him at the engagement party so it's not like we don't know each other. But with the way he's glaring at me, it's clear he's not thrilled to see me at Sasha's house this early in the morning. Maybe she had a point about not wanting anyone to know I'm here.

"Sasha hasn't been answering her phone. Kay was getting worried."

The first day, Sasha's phone had been ringing constantly. I knew that she'd called her family to let them know she wouldn't be coming by so I'd assumed that she'd called her friends, too.

"She's been sleeping a lot but she's feeling better now. I'm not sure if she's up to visitors though."

"Yet, you're here?" He raises an eyebrow.

Right. I'm not sure how to answer that so I focus on the basket in his hand. "You brought food?"

He looks down and then extends his arm, the dainty basket looking ridiculously small next to him. "Kay was worried about her being alone but I didn't want her to come and risk getting sick. It's just some blueberry muffins and a little container of macaroni and cheese that Kay made for her. It's Sasha's favorite."

"Comfort food. She's going to love this." I take the basket, unsure whether he's going to want to come in. His body language isn't the most welcoming but he hasn't done anything threatening. Yet.

He turns to go then stops and looks over his shoulder. "You're Tank's brother and that counts in your favor but Sasha is a friend. So if you're here for any reason other than the right ones, just be aware that I'm watching you. And I'm not the only one."

He turns and walks back down the drive, leaving me with a basket in my hands and a trash bag at my feet.

I walk back into the house and place the basket on the counter. It's early and Sasha probably won't wake up for a few hours. Especially since I kept her up late last night. Shame has my fist tightening around the edge of the counter. Sasha is a good girl, the kind that probably thought doggy style was inventive sex. My dick hardens just thinking about the prior night. I was demanding, barely giving her time to catch her breath between orgasms before I was working my way back inside her. No doubt she'll be sore today as well.

It would be all well and good if I were the kind of guy who sticks around. The boyfriend type who would run her a bath to soak her sore muscles and spend the day cuddling and reassuring her.

But Eli's visit just reminds me of the obvious. I'm not the boyfriend type and sticking around as long as I have is only going to make it harder when it's time to leave. Harder for Sasha. Even though she thinks she can handle a little fun between the sheets, she's not the type who can share her body and not her heart.

Worse, the more time I spend wrapped up in her world, with her sweet brand of affection, the harder it is for me to do the right thing: leave her alone.

* * * * *

It's been a long time since I've done this. I blow out a breath, eager to get this over with. While I'm waiting, I pull on a pair of thin black gloves. An image of Sasha, warm and cuddly in bed, runs through my mind. She's probably just waking up now. Soon she'll find my note.

Soon she'll hate me.

I shake my head, refusing to allow myself to second guess the first rational thing I've done since the day I met her. It's better she hates me than get hurt by someone aiming for me. What I'm about to do is further proof of how wrong I am for her.

A door slams across the street and I slide down further in my seat. Blade looks both ways up and down the street before he gets into the dark sedan parked at the curb. I don't move as he pulls out, keeping my head carefully averted as he passes by.

As soon as his car turns the corner, I open my door. After glancing in both directions, I cross the street quickly, keeping my eyes on the building before me. I'm on alert for any signs of movement or life. I've seen no indication that anyone but Blade is here but that's the kind of thing I can't afford to be wrong about.

As soon as I reach the side door, I pause, struck with a moment of doubt. This feels like so much more than just picking a lock. It's crossing a line, stepping back into waters I once swore I'd never enter again. But then I don't really have a choice, do I? Max has brought this fight to my doorstep and the only choice I have is to fight back in the only way I can. With information.

"You weren't kidding about being out of the game."

At the sudden voice at my side, I jump back, fists at the ready. "What the hell are you doing, Cole? You just scared the shit out of me."

"Didn't take much. I wasn't even trying to be quiet and I got the drop on you." Cole is dressed similarly in dark jeans with a black hoodie pulled up over his head. His slightly reddish hair looks darker than usual.

"Whatever." I fix him with a hard look. "Why are you here?"

"Call it curiosity. It was hard to get information on this dude. I figured you'd be by eventually."

His face gives nothing away but I've known Cole so long that his carefully blank expression provokes a sense of dread. Although I have to give him respect. He maintains steady eye contact as he lies to me. Just like he taught me to do.

"So you've got spies watching this place?"

He shrugs. "I've got spies everywhere."

I can only shake my head at the statement, knowing from experience how true it is, before I turn back to the door. The lock is old and presents little challenge. As soon as it clicks open, I cross the threshold and close the door silently behind us. It still looks like an old factory in here, with exposed beams and pipes in the ceilings and there's a general air of disuse about it. Once my eyes adjust to the dim lighting, I walk down the hallway to the left, opening doors and peering into each room.

The third door I open is the only room that looks like anyone has been here. There's a backpack, a pallet of blankets and a pillow in the corner directly on the concrete with a small stack of books next to it. I kneel next to the backpack and unzip it. There's a jumble of clothing and a small electronic game system which makes me smile.

The image of a scary guy like Blade playing video games is

highly amusing for some reason.

"Find anything?" Cole hangs back, content to let me do all the work.

"Nothing. This guy is like a ghost."

Frustrated, I zip the backpack and lean it against the wall exactly the way I found it. The books next to the bed are all classics. Nietzsche, Hemingway and there's even a copy of the Socratic Dialogues. The last book is in some language that I can't identify so I take a picture of it for Luke. I carefully pull back the bedding. Under the pillow there's a trio of knives with intricately carved designs on the hilts. They look brutal with deep, serrated edges. I cover them again, making sure to put everything back the way I found it.

I stand up, knowing my time is running out. I can't afford to have someone catch me here. But everything I've seen so far just makes the sick feeling in my stomach even worse.

Everything about this guy points to a career criminal type. He's smart enough to leave almost no trace of himself behind and without any clues to his identity I have no way to prepare for his next move.

We leave and I lock the door behind me carefully. The wind has picked up and trash blows by from one of the overturned cans down the street.

"Did you find what you were looking for?"

"Not really." My turmoil must show on my face because he cuffs me over the head affectionately, the same way he used to when I was a kid.

"If you ever need anything, you know where I am. We can

always use a pretty boy." He's still chuckling as he walks away.

There's a man a few yards away, so I keep my head down as I head back to my car.

Chapter Ten

Sasha

Usually waking up is a long process. I'm not a morning person, never have been, and waking up feels like slogging through quicksand with cement boots on. But today my eyes pop open instantly. I'm sore. Really sore. My thighs clench and I blush remembering why I feel so worked over. I turn to the other side of the bed, which is a mess of tangled sheets.

Empty.

I sit up slowly, pushing my hair out of my face. I forgot to tie it up last night so it's everywhere. Winding it around itself into a quick bun will have to do. I'm not up on morning after dos and don'ts but

I'm pretty sure letting your man see you looking like a hot mess isn't the way to go. After a quick visit to the bathroom to brush my teeth and wash my face, I pull on a robe and head down the hall to the kitchen. Gabe likes to get up early and check emails while he has his coffee. I've gotten used to the sight of him at my small kitchenette set, his large frame completely out of place in the dainty chairs.

But when I enter the kitchen, it's empty. Then I see the note on the counter and I just *know*. In an instant, my happy mood crashes and burns. I stand there for a minute, frozen in place, trying not to cry.

Finally I move forward and grab the note, reading it as I continue to the refrigerator. It says exactly what I expected, that he needed to get home and that he'll see me later.

In all fairness, there are probably a bunch of things he's been neglecting while he was here entertaining me. The whole time he was here, he only left once to pick up some clothes and a few things at the store. That's probably what turned my head and made me forget to keep my feelings in check. A man who grocery shops?

That's enough to make any woman fall in love.

My shoulders slump as I read the note again. The disappointment that I feel isn't even the worst part. It's the hurt. Gabe and I may not have a relationship but I at least thought we liked each other. Someone you like deserves more than a hastily written note on the counter. Even worse is that after spending so much time together, *I know Gabe*. I know how he thinks, how he withdraws emotionally when he doesn't want to talk about something. This is more than just a guy being a jerk after a one-night stand. He's running scared.

Which disappoints me more than I expected.

Over the next few days, I resolve to forget about Gabe which turns out to be much easier said than done. There's plenty to keep me busy between a new temp job doing admin work for a local law firm and poring over expenses for the club. But everything reminds me of him now and everywhere I turn, I keep imagining that I see his face. His memory is tormenting me and it kills me to admit the truth. It wasn't just fun and games with Gabe.

I miss him.

On Saturday morning the doorbell rings just as I'm stepping out of the shower. I grab at the towel on the rack, wrapping it hastily around my head to stop the water from dripping into my eyes.

Who could that be?

Kay called me yesterday to make sure I got the basket she sent, so she knows that I'm okay. She very carefully avoided any mention of the fact that Gabe was at my house but I could tell she was curious about what's going on between us.

The fact that she hasn't asked about it makes me think that Eli might have played a part in why Gabe left so quickly. I doubt I even want to know what Eli said to him. I sigh. Having family and friends who love you is a blessing but it comes with the assurance of them sticking their nose in your business and thinking they know more about what you need than you do. But if Gabe can be scared off from a few harsh words then he probably wasn't going to stick around anyway. I shake off the renewed sense of hurt as I pull my damp hair back into a ponytail and dress in my favorite pair of jeans and a frilly red blouse that makes me feel festive.

The doorbell rings again. With a curse, I walk up front, buttoning the blouse as I walk. Whoever it is clearly isn't going away.

"Who is it?" I yell out. I zip my jeans right before I reach the door.

"It's me. Gabe."

I rush to the door and then look through the peephole. Shock zips through me and then just as quickly, a rush of heat.

What is he doing back here?

My hand runs over my hair, ensuring none of my wild curls have escaped my ponytail holder. When I realize what I'm doing, I shove my vanity aside and open the door. Gabe spent days looking at me when I was either vomiting or sleeping. He's already seen me at my worst. At least I took a shower today. That's already an improvement.

"Hey! What are you doing here? Did you forget something?" The breezy, cheery tone of my voice sounds fake even to my ears but I'm determined not to let on that he hurt me.

When he looks up, my heart almost stops. Why does he have to be so handsome? I teased him when we first met, calling him pretty boy, but he really is masculine perfection from the sharp dominant lines of his cheekbones to those firm, perfectly shaped lips. God, even the way his thick dark hair flops over his forehead is sexy. It's seriously not fair that he looks like this when I'm working so hard to pretend he doesn't exist.

"I'm here for my music lesson." He lifts the strap of the guitar slung over his chest. Then he leans closer and whispers, "This is for the benefit of your nosy neighbors."

He steps in and closes the door behind him. Then he takes off the guitar and drops it on the couch. It lands with a muffled sound.

"Is there actually something in here? I thought you were just faking." I unzip the case, shocked to find that there really is a guitar inside. My mouth falls open. It's a Gibson.

"Yeah, it's one of Zack's. I figured he wouldn't mind."

I cover my mouth to keep from laughing. Gabe loves to tease his brother but in this case, I don't think he actually knows what he's done.

"Um, Gabe? This is a really expensive guitar. Did you ask him before you took it?"

He shrugs and takes a bite out of one of the muffins from Kay's gift basket. "I haven't seen him play it in a long time so I figured it was one he wouldn't miss."

I stroke a finger over the strings. "You are crazy, you know that? Your brother is going to be pissed."

He walks over and taps me on the nose. "I'm willing to take that risk. I wanted to check on you."

His eyes are warm as he looks me over. I have to resist the urge to fidget under his gaze. It was strange enough having him in my house for days on end but to have him show up out of the blue because he's worried about me? It makes me feel things, things that

158

bring me a shade too close to caring about him. I can't allow that to happen. It's definitely not a smart move on my part to allow myself to fall for someone who has been clear that he has no intention of falling back.

"I'm fine. Feeling much better. Now that I'm not contagious I'm going to visit my sister, Brenna. She's been worried about me and after the way we left things ... Well, I want her to know there's no hard feelings. Maybe they don't think I'm an entrepreneur but we're still family. I don't want this to come between us."

"That's good. I have to get back. I should probably put that guitar back before Zack notices it's gone."

"That would be a good idea."

He slings the guitar case over his shoulder again. As we walk back to the front door, my eyes roam over him greedily, taking in every detail. I got spoiled seeing him days on end. I'm probably going through Gabe withdrawal and that's why I'm fighting the urge to invent a reason for him to stay. But I know I can't.

"It was sweet of you to come check on me but you really didn't need to do that. I could use a little space after ... everything."

Hopefully he can read between the lines. I don't regret what happened. My body is still humming from the things he did to me so I could never regret it. But it's better that I don't get too used to having him here. Nothing good can come of that. As much fun as I had spending time with him, I have to accept the fact that he's not mine to keep.

Just before he opens the door, he leans over and kisses me on the cheek. "I missed talking to you."

Then he pulls the door open and leaves without looking back.

* * * * *

One of the most pure joys in life is the sound of a child's laughter. I have to cover my ears part of the time as my nephew runs past squealing, wearing nothing but a Superman T-shirt and a diaper. Brenna looks up when he runs through the room again and then shakes her head.

"I hear screams even in my sleep. I get no peace around here." She smiles faintly as she says it though, nonchalantly turning another page of the magazine in her lap.

"Let me know if you and Evan need a night out. Aunt Sasha is always happy to help out. You know I love spending time with him."

"And he loves you. You're going to be such an awesome mom someday. Speaking of moms, ours is on her way over. Evan kept hinting that he wanted an apple pie so Mom made him one. I swear, she spoils him just like she does her grandson."

"I guess I should go then." My parents visited me when I was sick but Mom was distracted by fussing over me. Now that things are back to normal, any interaction with my mom will revert back to her usual questions about my personal life and career, or in her opinion, my lack thereof. My mom loves me, I know she does, but I can't handle a motherly interrogation right now.

Brenna rolls her eyes. "Sasha, you know she means well. We just want you to be happy. Find a nice guy, have a steady job. You know, start living your life."

"I am living my life, Bren. Even if my life doesn't look like yours, that doesn't mean it's not valid."

She sits back and closes the magazine. "You know what I mean."

I clamp my lips shut to block the angry words that threaten to spill out. This is a familiar argument and every time we both spout the same words and end up upset. There's no point to hashing out the same things over and over. We have very different ideas about what my life should look like.

"Look, I know you guys have been worried about me. After the show—" A sudden rush of emotion steals my voice and I reach over to take a sip from the glass of iced tea on the coffee table to soothe my suddenly scratchy throat. Thinking about that day, the single most humiliating day of my life, will never be easy.

"After the show, I was a mess. I know I was. But I'm fine now and I've got a plan to get myself back on track. Maybe I'm not meant to tour the country and perform in front of large crowds but I've always enjoyed performing in smaller venues. I have a plan to open the club on time and I've even gotten a few new investors." I don't bother telling her that the new investors are Dad and Uncle Tommy.

Brenna looks surprised. "Really? That's wonderful. But I'm not worried about your career, I'm worried about you. You deserve to be with a great guy and not these losers you normally pick. I can't believe that fool Chaz had the nerve to dump you right before the show. Bastard."

"I haven't even thought of him at all."

She falls silent. Then gasps. "You have a new boyfriend and you didn't tell me?"

"No, I don't." But even as I say it, I flush and Brenna knows me too well to let that pass.

"Okay, what's wrong with this one?"

I wrinkle my nose at her. "It's nothing. It's just … what would you have done if Evan hadn't wanted anything serious?"

Brenna pauses, a thoughtful look on her face. "I don't know. I guess that depends on why he was keeping me at a distance. Is he not attracted to me?"

"He's definitely attracted." Physical chemistry has never been an issue with Gabe.

"Then it probably means he's got something going on in his personal life. That's a tough one because I hate to think that I would have just let Evan go without even fighting for him."

"So you think I should fight?" Her answer means more to me than I'm willing to admit.

"I'm never a big fan of trying to push people where they don't want to go. But there's nothing wrong with making a man an offer is there? Just watch it because that's how I got that one." She gestures to Carter as he runs past screaming again.

We laugh and start talking about other things. But in the back of my mind, I'm wondering if I dare risk pushing Gabe. Pushing him for more might mean pushing him away.

* * * * *

That evening, Brenna's words are still running through my mind, but I have to push them aside because I have a gig. Usually, I look forward to this all month. Singing is the only thing that makes me feel alive sometimes. Even when I'm tired, even when I'm stressed, being on stage and letting music flow through me is my favorite thing in the world.

But tonight, I'm just not feeling it.

Crooning the second verse of *My Funny Valentine,* I look out over the crowded ballroom of the Piedmont Hotel at the elegant crowd. When Finn told me he knew the owner of the Piedmont, Ethan Marks, I'd been amazed. Their jazz night is legendary. Upscale. They only hire the best and even then Ethan has a reputation for being picky. I figured he gave me a chance because he's friends with Finn but friendship only goes so far. It honestly never occurred to me that I would actually get this gig.

Performing here is usually the highlight of my month. Instead, I'm struggling to get through until I can go back home and curl up in my pajamas.

The crowd shifts and that's when I see him. I momentarily stumble over the words I know so well. I blink and then he's gone, the crowd shifting again, swallowing up the gentleman in the striking midnight blue tuxedo. I finish off the song, grateful that it's the last of my set. Thoughts of Gabe have been distracting me all day and now I'm imagining that I see him everywhere.

Then I step off stage and he's there.

Gabe holds out a hand to help me down the stairs and I accept it out of shock more than anything else. I smile as I pass Ethan, who nods in approval before continuing his conversation with the man he's talking to. Keeping my eyes straight ahead, I refuse to acknowledge Gabe again. I just told him that I need space and now he shows up here? I don't believe for one minute that it's a coincidence. Damn him for how he throws me off guard!

Gabe speeds up until he's walking by my side. I walk faster, desperate to reach the bar.

The bartender, Clary, hands over my usual drink as soon as I arrive. "Vodka tonic."

"You are a saint." I take a sip and then groan when Gabe leans against the bar next to me.

"I've never seen you sing before. You sing the same way you do everything else. With everything you have. It was incredible."

Every part of me blooms under his attention. I hate that I'm so parched for his attention, drinking up every drop of his admiration like it's the sustenance I've been waiting for.

"Why are you here, Gabe?"

"I had to see you."

"We had a great time and I don't regret it. You're the one who ran out the next morning. So I repeat, why are you here?"

He grabs my arm and pulls me closer, turning his back to the other people standing at the bar. "This entire week all I could think of was you. I came to see you this morning because I thought that would be enough. Just a quick visit to stop this … obsession. But it's not enough."

164

As he speaks, he's looking at me with this savage expression that I've never seen on him before. The intensity is almost too much to take. It's as if he's trying to soothe the beast within with the object of its torment.

"Nothing will ever be enough," he whispers.

I suck in a breath as our eyes meet and something tightens in my stomach. Just like that, it's back, the same powerful awareness of him that makes me want to claw his clothes off.

His words should soothe me. It should be a relief to hear that I'm not the only one who feels this pull, this overwhelming sense of losing control of who am I when he's near but it only makes me feel worse.

Because in all the things he's said, how he wants me and how he's obsessed with me, nowhere in all of that speech did he say he wants to feel this way. The way he feels is like a disease that he's trying to shake and for me, it's like a flame that I'm drawn to. A flame that warms me, thrills me and makes me long to get burned.

Suddenly he jerks back and pats his pocket. When he moves his hand, I can hear his phone vibrating. After several rings it stops and then immediately starts again.

"Something important?" Part of me is hoping it is so I can have a reprieve from this maddening conversation.

He withdraws it from the inner pocket of his suit jacket. After glancing at the screen briefly, he shuts it off. "Nothing is more important than this."

"What do you want from me, Gabe?"

"I want you. That's the only thing I know."

"You tell me we can't be together then you say we'll be friends. We have an amazing night but then you run away. I don't think you know what you want."

My head is spinning. Being with him feels like standing on the edge of a cliff. It'll only take one strong wind to send me soaring and while I might enjoy the ride, I already know I can't survive the crash landing.

He sighs. "That was an asshole move, I admit. But something reminded me that I'm not good for you."

"So what changed?" My voice breaks and that's the first time I see a hint of the real Gabe, *my Gabe*, in his face.

He cradles my face in his hands and smiles down at me gently. "I realized that I can't stay away from you and I'm not noble enough to try anymore."

Chapter Eleven

Gabe

Sasha runs a hand over the fabric of my bedspread and looks over at me nervously. Convincing her to come home with me was the easy part. What to do with her now that she's here is an entirely different matter.

She affects me like no one else, that much has been apparent from the moment we met and it leaves me at a loss. It's crazy to think that I can suddenly turn into the kind of guy who deserves a girl like her but at the same time, I know I can't let her go.

For someone like me, who has always gotten through life with a mixture of bravado and manipulation, Sasha represents an irresistible lure. The one woman who can see through me. The one woman that makes me want to truly be myself with her. No manipulation. No lies.

She also represents my worst fear. That without my usual game, I won't be able to keep her with me.

I dial Luke's number again. It goes straight to voicemail. Maybe I should have gone to his place instead of coming home. But in the heat of the moment, all I wanted was to get Sasha on my turf.

She sits up straighter when I sit on the edge of the bed next to her. I don't think she could be any more jumpy and it's completely charming. As bubbly as she is, I would have never guessed she'd be this uncomfortable just by being in my bedroom.

"Did you get in touch with Luke?" She grabs the edge of the coverlet and scrunches it into a ball.

"Not yet. He's not the type to ignore me so he probably turned his phone off. I left a message with his mom at the bakery and she promised to tell him as soon as he shows up."

We both fall silent and there's no sound except for the shallow rasp of her breathing and the soft scratch of her nails as she yanks at the covers.

Part of me wants to tell her to relax but then I glance behind me at the bed. It's probably not a great idea for either of us to get too comfortable. If I don't get myself under control I'll have her on her back with her ankles by my ears and that's not why I brought her here. We're supposed to be talking. Figuring things out. I glance over at the neckline of her emerald green evening gown. It dips low

168

enough for me to see the curves of her breasts and the rich color highlights the deep tone of her skin. *Christ, we'd better talk fast.*

"Hey Gabe, I thought you were going—"

The door to my room flies open and Zack walks in. When he catches sight of Sasha, he stops abruptly. For a moment he just stares at her. Then he says, "Oh ... hey."

Sasha looks like she wants to die. "Hi, Zack."

I stand and grab Zack by the arm. My brother has a tendency to blurt out the first thing he's thinking and considering the situation, Sasha might run off if he says the wrong thing.

"Come on." I drag him into the hall. He looks at me, a silly little smile on his face. One that makes me want to turn around and walk back into the room.

"Don't look at me like that. It's not what you think." Then I think about the situation objectively. There's a gorgeous woman in my room that I have every intention of getting naked. "Well, it's not entirely what you think."

"It never is. Besides, I like her."

Zack leans in the doorway and waves at Sasha. With the appreciative way he's looking at her I just bet he does like her. I slap a hand in the middle of his forehead and pull him back into the hall.

"Okay, enough of that. What are we, twelve?"

"You are." Zack smirks.

"I'll see you later. Much later."

"Got it." Zack heads for the staircase and I go back into the room with Sasha. She gives me an amused look as I sit on the bed again.

"You could have let him come in and say hi. I really like talking to Zack."

I grit my teeth. "He really likes talking to you, too. And looking at you. As a matter of fact I think he likes looking at you a little too much for my taste."

Sasha giggles and my annoyance vanishes. "I love to hear that sound."

Her smile fades slightly. "What sound?"

"You. Laughing. You should always be happy."

Voices in the hall cut off whatever she was about to say and I have to suppress the urge to go throttle my brother. I stand and open the door. Then I rear back in surprise at the sight of Luke.

"What are you doing here?"

Sasha appears in the doorway behind me. "I can go if you guys need to talk."

I turn around and anchor an arm around her waist. "No! Stay. Please. Let's go downstairs and you can relax with a glass of wine while Luke and I talk."

Luke looks completely shell-shocked and I remember then Finn's hilarious retelling of the first time he introduced Sasha to our youngest brother. Apparently he has a little crush. When I look over at Sasha, my chest tightens. I definitely can't fault my little brother for his taste.

As we walk downstairs, Sasha tries to make small talk with Luke but he's clammed up completely. Eventually she gives up. Once downstairs, I lead her to an overstuffed chair in the living room.

"I'll bring you a glass of wine. Luke, you want a beer?"

He nods absently and perches on the edge of the couch. I smother a laugh and then enter the kitchen. Zack looks up.

"Did Luke find you?" He snickers and ducks when I try to punch his arm.

"Yeah, although you should definitely warn me next time. He might rethink his decision to get to know us if he walks in on me with his dream girl."

I pass him three beers and then uncork the bottle of white wine that I keep on hand in case one of our moms drops by. I pour a generous glass and carry it out to Sasha who takes a big gulp before standing up.

"Where's your restroom? I have to get these pins out of my hair."

I point her to the bathroom off the kitchen.

She waves over her shoulder at the others. "Excuse me for a minute, guys. I'll be right back."

As soon as she's gone, I turn to Luke. "So what's up?"

He accepts the beer that Zack holds out. "Uh, well, that picture you sent me of Blade's stuff? The language in the book is Gaelic. It explains why I haven't found anything through my usual sources if this guy is from overseas. Actually that's why I was trying to get in touch with you. We need to get into Interpol files."

The more we find out about Blade, the less we seem to really know. "Interpol, huh? You can't get in there?"

"It's not whether I can do it. Of course I can do it." Luke makes a disgusted sound and rolls his eyes.

Zack coughs next to me, covering his laugh and even I'm amused at the affronted look on Luke's face. *Who knew geek egos were so fragile?*

"Right. So, what's the problem then?"

"The problem is that it's not worth the heat that could bring. If you have any friends with access to Interpol files, doing it legally is better."

Zack glances over at me. "I'm sure Tank can figure something out."

Sasha comes back then and the conversation turns to more generic things. She starts telling us about her gig at the Piedmont. After a few minutes she has us all laughing describing her audition with the owner and how nervous she was. Her hair was in some sort of elegant updo when she was onstage but she's taken that down and her hair cascades over her shoulders in long waves. As beautiful as she looks, I find I miss her natural wild curls. It reminds me of how she looked when I made love to her. She turns to me and her voice falters, probably because she recognizes the look in my eyes. She flushes and her hands start playing with the ends of her hair before her eyes meet mine again.

Yeah, you know what you do to me, beautiful girl.

A half an hour later, Luke is gone and Zack has finally decided to make himself scarce. He keeps saying that he's going to get his own place and every time I remind him that there's no rush. Now I find myself wishing I had rushed him a little bit. Watching Sasha walk up the stairs, her curvy bottom just a few inches in front of me, has me on edge. I can't help thinking that it's going to be a lot harder to spread her out and do all the things I want to do to her with my brother right down the hall.

In my room, I close the door behind us and turn the lock. At the quiet sound, Sasha's eyes meet mine. The innocent expression on her face doesn't fool me at all. As she moves closer, I take a deep breath, bracing for whatever outrageous thing she's going to do. Then she stands on tiptoe and kisses me on the cheek.

It's so innocent but I can feel my body heating up as she presses kisses to my face, neck and ears before coming back to my mouth, our tongues twining together in a way that has me hard and ready in an instant. Her hand travels down, gliding over my abs and I know exactly where she's headed. I sit down on the bed because my legs are unsteady as hell. She stands in front of me and tugs at the top button of my pants.

"This really isn't why I brought you here, I swear. I wanted us to talk. To … talk about something." My mind is quickly turning to mush and I let out a low rumble of displeasure when she pulls back.

"No, you're right. We do need to talk." After a few deep breaths, she sits next to me. Just looking at her sitting there with her hair spilling over her shoulders and her brown eyes soft with desire makes me lose my breath.

"Don't listen to me. I'm an idiot, we can talk later." I reach for her and she evades my grasp with a soft laugh.

"Gabe, we do need to set up some ground rules. That's where we went wrong last time. If we do this, you have to promise no more freaking out afterward."

I shove a hand through my hair. "You're right."

She climbs atop me and grasps my face in her hands. "Look, the way we feel is sudden and intense but it doesn't have to be scary. I'm not looking for anything serious right now either. Let's just keep this casual. I need to focus on the club and my singing career. I really like you. I don't see why we can't just enjoy each other. Right?"

Everything she's saying should make me feel better but strangely the idea of Sasha sharing my bed and feeling nothing for me leaves me hollow. Which makes no sense. A gorgeous woman who wants to enjoy pleasure without expecting a proposal is everything I should want.

Isn't it?

She's still waiting for me to respond so I nod, mutely. Her face brightens and she pulls me closer for a soft kiss.

"Good. Now it's time for me to enjoy you naked." Then she rips the front of my dress shirt wide open and shoves me back on the bed.

* * * * *

Waking up with someone is a totally new experience. I know what Sasha thinks, that I've had a legion of women traipsing in and out of my bedroom, but I've never brought anyone into my bed before. Sex was about adventure and risk. Screwing in dark corners at clubs, in the car or even outside was more my style. A bed was fine as long as it wasn't mine. I wasn't really interested in the intimacy of sharing sleeping space with anyone.

Until now.

After ripping my shirt off last night, she'd entertained herself by exploring every inch of my chest with her mouth. She seemed to enjoy being in charge and I had no problem letting her take advantage of me. I had shown considerable restraint in letting her do things her way until I'd finally flipped her over and taken her from behind. We'd both come violently, Sasha biting down on my thumb to keep from screaming. When I saw the little bruises on her hips, I'd been worried that I'd used her too hard. Sasha had reassured me that she was fine but it shook me, seeing those marks. Then I realized that maybe a part of me was trying to mark her.

She's sure as hell left her mark on me.

I glance over at her. She's cuddled up into a little ball, her hands pillowed under her cheek. Her hair is in wild disarray around her head and I know she's going to immediately want to tame it when she wakes up. I savor seeing her a little messy. The dark shadows that were under her eyes a few weeks ago have faded. She looks so peaceful. I'd never have thought that making someone else smile could so quickly become the focus of my whole world. But slowly, Sasha has infiltrated every aspect of my life. She fits into my zany family and she likes me.

The simplicity of that stuns me through and through. Even with everything she knows about me, who I am and what I've done, she likes me. She believes in me. And she makes me want to be a better man.

I move the covers back slightly, moving slowly so I won't disturb her. I pull on a pair of jeans and T-shirt and with one last glance back at Sasha, I make my way downstairs.

Zack is at the breakfast bar hunched over a bowl of cereal. "Hey. I noticed Sasha's car was still in the drive. It's not having any problems, is it?"

"No. She stayed over last night. She's still asleep."

His eyes widen slightly. Being under his gaze makes me feel antsy, so I start rooting around in the pantry, finally pulling out a box of dry cereal. I pop a handful in my mouth and lean against the counter. Zack raps his knuckles against the granite surface to get my attention.

His eyes are solemn as he says, "I'm really happy for you, man. She's amazing."

I crunch loudly on another handful of cereal, uncomfortable with the serious tone of the conversation. "She just crashed here last night, dude. I didn't say we're getting married."

His serious expression doesn't change. "You didn't have to. The fact that she's here says it all. And it's a good thing."

"Isn't this a little heavy for Sunday morning conversation?" Although I understand what he means, it makes me feel even more like a fraud. He thinks I'm stepping up to the plate, giving Sasha the serious commitment she deserves when I'm just another guy taking advantage of her trusting nature. Because if she knew the truth about me, she definitely wouldn't be upstairs wrapped in my blankets.

"I'm serious, Gabe. You deserve to be happy."

"Do I?" I don't have to qualify the statement. Zack knows who and what I am. What I'm capable of. He knows just how far I'm willing to go past any lines of morality when I want something.

Zack looks like he's about to say something else but before he can, his attention suddenly snaps to something over my shoulder.

"Morning."

I turn at the sound of Sasha's voice. She's wearing my dress shirt with the sleeves rolled up and a pair of my boxer shorts. Under my gaze she blushes slightly and tugs at the bottom of the shirt.

"I hope you don't mind." She glances over at Zack before her eyes come back to me, as if she's not sure how to act in front of him.

I move around the counter and pull her into my arms for a quick kiss. Afterward, she breaks into a wide smile.

"Of course I don't mind. It looks way better on you. Do you want some breakfast? We don't have much other than eggs."

"Eggs are perfect." Sasha accepts the coffee mug that Zack hands her and then pours herself a cup from the pot on the counter.

Zack sits again and then looks over at me. "You going in to the shop today? A friend of mine asked me to take a look at her carburetor. I didn't get a chance to do it yesterday."

The way he says *friend* tells me that he's doing it for some girl.

"I probably should. I need to catch up on some paperwork."

Zack nods. "Better you than me. You should come with us Sasha."

I have the refrigerator open and freeze with my hand on the carton of eggs. What the hell is Zack doing? Sasha isn't the type of girl who wants to hang around in an auto-shop with a bunch of guys.

177

Awkward silence descends and Sasha shakes her head. "I should probably get going pretty soon. I have some stuff to do."

"It would be fun. I'd much rather look at you than this guy's ugly mug." Zack points at me.

Sasha takes a small sip from her cup, eyeing me over the rim. "Honestly, he's prettier than me."

Of course, that has Zack howling with laughter. He gets up and pulls Sasha into a hug. "Please come entertain me. Don't leave me alone with this stick in the mud and a bunch of horny old men."

Laughing she hugs him back. "I'm sure Gabe has a lot of stuff he needs to get done today. I wouldn't want to get in the way."

Something about the way she says it makes my hand pause in the act of cracking the eggs into the skillet. She looks uncertain. Then I remember our rules last night. Keep things casual. I hope she didn't think that meant she has to make herself scarce every time we have sex.

I abandon the skillet on the stove so I can look her directly in the eyes. "Sasha, you are never in the way. Ever. I want you to come. I was hoping that you'd hang out with me today. I didn't even get to give you a full tour of the house yet."

At my words, she gives a little nod. "Well, I really can't anyway because I don't have anything to wear."

Zack speaks up, looking over at me mischievously. "Wear something of Josie's. She's got a ton of stuff here."

When Sasha's face closes up, I want to strangle him. "She stays over sometimes when she can't deal with her folks. All her stuff is in the *guest room*." I emphasize the words while glaring at Zack.

"I'm sure she doesn't want some random chick wearing her stuff," Sasha protests.

"Good thing you're not some random chick then."

After a quick breakfast of eggs and toast, I lead her upstairs before Zack can stir up any more shit. She comes down ten minutes later in a pair of jeans that are slightly too loose and a blue sweater. Her hair is bundled up on top of her head in some kind of complicated knot.

"I'm ready to go."

After grabbing our coats, we head outside. Sasha flips up her hood as a defense against the brisk wind. Once settled in the passenger seat of the car, she looks over at me.

"I really don't mind staying in the car while you do whatever you need to do."

"Why would you stay in the car?"

She shakes her head slightly. "I just don't want you to feel obligated. I know Zack sort of pushed you into inviting me but we're just hanging out, remember? I don't expect you to introduce me to everyone you know. No expectations."

"I don't feel obligated. I want you to meet the rest of our crew. They're a bit rough around the edges but they're good guys." The thought that she feels like I don't want her with me is so far from reality that I'm not sure how she even arrived at that conclusion. If anything, I want her with me way more than I should. We're supposed to be keeping things casual but I want her to be at home in every part of my world.

She smiles and nods. As I pull out of the driveway, I can feel her sneaking glances over at me.

I park in the back lot behind the shop. As soon as we enter, Jim looks up from the computer in the back office.

"Good, you're here. The inventory is fucked up again."

"Uh, Jim. This is Sasha."

At the sight of her, Jim stands a little straighter. "Beg your pardon, miss."

Sasha just laughs. "I remember you. You were the one who towed my car."

He extends a hand and pumps hers heartily. "That's right. I'm usually the one that goes on the runs if I'm here."

I motion toward Jim. "He's also the only reason Zack and I have a shop. He's the one who taught us about cars."

Jim cackles. "Only after I caught you both trying to steal mine. Little bastards." He glances over at Sasha again.

She clamps her lips together and I can tell she's trying not to laugh. "So you caught him trying to steal your car? How did you go from catching a thief to teaching them how to fix cars?"

Jim grins, revealing a row of crooked teeth. "I figured teaching them how to do something useful was better than letting 'em get hauled off to jail. My old man wasn't around a lot when I was a kid either so I know how it is. Plus, I was a little sweet on Debbie back then. Gabe's momma has always been a looker."

I clap him on the back, halting his story. "Okay, that's enough about that."

Jim nods to us both as we continue up front. One of my mechanics, Reed Harris, looks up as we enter the front of the shop. He's in the reception area making a cup of coffee. After more introductions and Reed sending me an impressed look when Sasha isn't looking, I lead her into my office. There are a few new client accounts that I need to update and I also have to check the upcoming payroll to make sure everyone's hours look right. When I look up, Sasha is watching me.

"Sorry, I know this is boring. That's why I thought it was weird for Zack to invite you. Hanging out in an auto garage doesn't seem like it would be your thing."

"Are you kidding? I'm already thinking of all the stuff you can show me here. I saw a motorcycle in there. Can you teach me to ride? Then we could race!"

She gets excited about the strangest things. I'm willing to bet that she was a handful as a kid. I have a vision of a gorgeous little girl that has me wrapped around her finger the same way Sasha does. The clarity of the image stuns me almost as much as how badly I want that. It takes me off guard, this sudden longing for all the things I never imagined I'd want. Security. Stability. Family.

Shaken, I cover my reaction with a forced smile. "Sasha, we're not racing motorcycles."

She sticks out her tongue and then jumps up. "Maybe Zack will do it!"

I watch in astonishment as she races out the door. By the time I catch up to her, she's behind the front desk where Reed is picking up the keys for the next vehicle he's going to work on.

He grins down at her. "Did you lose something, boss?"

"I hope not."

She gives me a cheeky grin. "Don't let me distract you. I know you need to get some paperwork done. I don't mind waiting."

My first instinct is to protest but I know I won't be able to focus if she's in my office. "Okay, I only need fifteen minutes and then we can go."

I hate to leave her with nothing to do but I really do need to get stuff done. Besides, how much trouble can she get into in fifteen minutes?

With a nod of thanks to Reed, I walk back to my office. As soon as the door closes I hear, "Okay, now we can get to the fun stuff. You can show me how to hotwire a car!"

And I can't keep the smile off my face.

Chapter Twelve

Sasha

Monday morning, I move back and survey the table that I've just assembled. After the initial suggestions Gabe had given me about reducing my budget, I'd been confident enough to start ordering furniture. Keeping costs under control is really important but I couldn't resist splurging on a few things. The scarred wood tables invoke the look of an old school speakeasy. They look so good that I dance a little jig.

"Performing already?"

At the sound of the amused voice behind me, I halt mid-booty shake. Busted, I turn around slowly to see Gabe standing in the doorway behind me holding a large brown paper bag.

"I totally knew you were there."

He snorts. "Right. I brought you lunch but please don't let me interrupt you. I was enjoying the view."

Coyly, I give a little shimmy and dance my way over to him seductively. Gratified at the slack-jawed expression on his face, I snatch the bag from his hand.

"I'm starving!"

He growls and then grabs me from behind. "You can have the food but I need my daily dose of Sasha." Then he buries his face in my neck and plants a soft kiss behind my ear.

Just like that, I melt. Oh the things this man does to me!

Suddenly breathless, I clutch the bag tighter. "Thank you for bringing me lunch. You didn't have to do that."

He circles one of the tables. "I wanted to see you. And I wanted to see your new stuff. It looks good."

"Yeah, it does, doesn't it? Sit down, try it out."

He obediently takes a seat, stretching his long legs beneath the table. Excitement bursts through me again. Somehow having someone else here makes it all seem real.

Gabe unpacks the food, which turns out to be sub sandwiches and little containers of potato salad. While we're eating, he listens to my ideas for decorating the club once all the furniture has been delivered.

"I wish I had a magical team of genies to build the stage."
There's an intense satisfaction in doing things on my own but after

the time and effort it took to unpack today's delivery, I'm starting to think it's going to take a miracle for me to pull this off. It's not just the money, it's the sheer physical effort required to put everything into place. I thought I was in decent shape but I'm already exhausted!

Gabe gives me a measured look. "If you want, I could probably do it. I'm pretty handy."

"I bet you could. Is there anything you can't do? No, don't answer that."

He grins and finishes off the last bite of his sandwich. As he wipes his hands on a napkin, I suppress a little pang of sadness that our lunch date is almost over. After this, it'll be back to assembling the rest of the tables on my own. The one thing I hadn't counted on was how lonely it can be doing all of this by myself.

After gathering up the wrappings and empty containers from our lunch, Gabe grabs my hand. "Seriously, Sasha if you need anything, I'm more than happy to help."

"I know. But I really want to do this on my own. It's my project and I need to feel like I'm doing it on my own steam."

"Stubborn girl. Stubborn beautiful girl." But he squeezes my hand in understanding.

"Besides, maybe I don't need a stage. Maybe my performers will move throughout the crowd and sing directly to the audience. It'll be an interactive show. Kind of like those cool flash mobs you see online where everyone is singing and dancing together." I do a little turn and spin away from him like a ballerina.

When I turn around, Gabe is watching me with the strangest

185

expression. "You are remarkable. Nothing keeps you down for long, does it?"

The open affection in his voice warms me through and through. He doesn't seem to expect an answer, just pulls me into his arms. He holds me for a long time and I have the sudden urge to clamp my arms around him. To never let him go.

But then he just kisses me on the forehead and says, "Lock up behind me, okay?"

* * * * *

About ten minutes after I get home that evening, the doorbell rings. I was all geared up for a night of conditioning my hair and eating leftovers since Gabe already warned me he's working late tonight. We're supposed to be casual so I hadn't let on that I was disappointed. But I was. And worried that maybe I'm more into this than he is.

Taking my sister's advice and presenting Gabe with an offer he couldn't refuse was always a risky prospect. Pretending that I'm okay with a casual thing hasn't been easy. But the way he acted today, the way he held me … wasn't so casual. I shiver remembering. Maybe he's been thinking about me all day, too? I skip to the door. Maybe he decided to ditch work and come over anyway!

But when I look through the peephole, I see the last two people I was expecting. I yank open the door.

"Kay? Eli? What are you guys doing here? Were we supposed to meet?"

Usually I'm not the forgetful type but with everything that's been going on lately it's possible that I spaced when we were making plans. I'd noticed a missed call from Kay earlier today but I'd been so exhausted that I'd figured I'd call her back this evening.

"No, I just wanted to come by." She doesn't meet my eyes as they come in. I shut the door behind them and turn around. Usually Kay comes right in and gets comfortable on the couch. Today she's standing awkwardly in the middle of the living room and hasn't even taken her coat off.

Something is wrong.

"Okay, what's going on?"

Kay wrings her hands. "I came by your new space around noon today. I wanted to take you to lunch."

"You did? Why didn't you come in?" Then it hits me that I was busy at noon. *Having lunch with Gabe.* Suddenly her discomfort makes sense. Depending on when she came by she could have seen something completely innocent or something completely ... *not.*

"I tried to stay out of it." Kay glances over at Eli.

He takes over. "When Tank asked me to find his youngest brother, I did a little digging on all of them. I wasn't trying to be nosy but I figured that there might be something that connected them that would help me find Luke. Well, the things I discovered about Gabe were troubling. I wasn't going to say anything but when Kay mentioned seeing you together today, I figured you'd want to know."

"Troubling?"

"He's got a clean record as an adult but there were a few

incidents that didn't add up for me. So I took a look into his juvenile records. It didn't take long to figure out the guy's a grifter."

"Not sure what that means but if you're trying to tell me he's a thief, I already know. He told me."

"*He told you?*" they ask in unison.

Kay recovers from her shock first. "Okay, well that's good that he's not hiding anything. But I couldn't help but worry."

I contemplate just telling her the truth but I'm honestly not sure how to explain what I'm doing with Gabe. It's not that I think she'll try to stop me but I know she's already worried about me getting hurt. So I go with a modified version of the truth.

"Gabe has been helping me out a lot with the business. It's really not a big deal." I don't mention the incredible sex or the fact that my heart turns over in my chest every time I see him. Kay will just worry needlessly.

As expected, my words seem to calm her. "Well, good. Anyway, I know you keep saying you're on a dating strike but I told Eli about my plan to fix you up and he thinks Maddox might be a good match. I don't think you've ever met him but he's worked for Eli for years. He's good looking, too. I think you'll like him."

"Good looking?" Eli repeats.

Kay rolls her eyes and waves him away. "Divorced but you know that's to be expected when you like older men."

Words can't even begin to describe how awkward this is. Eli is not the type of guy with the patience for gossip so I'm not sure how she got him to listen to the tales of my troubles. He looks completely uncomfortable.

"Kay, I'm sure Eli has way better things to do than worry about my social life."

Normally Eli is pretty reserved so I'm shocked when he suddenly leans closer. "You are my baby's best friend. I want you to be happy. And any guy that hurts you is going to be on my shit list. I'd rather just introduce you to some guys that I know have their heads on right."

I'm touched by his concern but simultaneously mortified. "You really don't have to do that."

If only they knew that my stay single plan is already in jeopardy because I can't keep my thoughts, or hands, away from Gabe.

Eli seems to understand that I'm uncomfortable. Probably because he really doesn't want to talk about this either.

"The option is always open. I'll leave you two ladies to talk." He pulls out his cell phone and moves to the other side of the room.

I turn back to Kay. She's digging in her purse. Finally she finds what she's looking for, which turns out to be a small bag of potato chips. When she feels the heat of my gaze, she looks up. "What?"

"I can't believe you told Eli. Don't you guys have better things to talk about than me? Like the newest sex toys on the market or something."

Kay was initially a little freaked out when she discovered that her hunky future hubby was into some of the more adventurous things in the bedroom. However, she quickly discovered that having an inventive and creative man in your bed is not something to fear.

"Not lately." Kay looks miserable. "Things aren't as perfect as they seem. He hasn't touched me in weeks."

"Is he worried about hurting you? Some guys are weird about sex during pregnancy. Every time I see you guys, he's telling you to put your feet up or to relax. If he thinks standing is too taxing for you, he's probably afraid to touch you."

Kay stills and then her eyes swing to mine. The guilty look on her face says it all. "I was going to tell you after my first doctor's appointment. Damn Eli and his meddling!"

I laugh. "Kay, that wasn't what gave it away. You think I can't tell when my bestie has a bun in the oven? I was there for the first round of pregnancy cravings, remember?" I point at the package of chips that she's inhaling.

She crumples the now empty package in her fist and sighs. "I'm even hungrier than I was with Hope. I'm trying to keep it under control so I won't gain so much weight this time. I don't want Eli to feel like he's marrying a cow."

"Eli loves you and you are going to be a gorgeous bride. I'm totally jealous of the way he looks at you."

She glances over at me. "I am pretty lucky, huh?"

"You know you are. But then again, so is he."

"That's what it's about. Finding someone who makes you feel like you won the lottery. You always date these guys who don't appreciate you. I think you do it to stay in control. You need to meet someone who isn't intimidated by you but will challenge you."

Her words make me a little sad. "But what if I meet that guy and the challenge is too much?"

Eli appears at her elbow. "Sorry to interrupt but I need to get back."

Kay's eyes narrow and for a moment I'm sure she's going to ask me to explain that cryptic statement. Then she smiles and turns to Eli. "It's okay. I think we've meddled enough for one day."

*   *   *   *   *

The things Eli told me stay on my mind long after they leave. Even though I know Gabe has changed, I wonder what got him into stealing cars in the first place. It doesn't fit with the things I know about him. The way he's so protective of his family and the way he took care of me when I was sick. It's so hard to reconcile that with a guy who stole cars and almost ended up in jail.

When Gabe shows up the next evening, I think he can tell that I have a lot on my mind. He settles back on the couch to watch television while I put a dish of baked chicken breasts in the oven. I set the timer and then drop down on the opposite end of the couch. He reaches over and pulls my feet into his lap.

"Rough day?"

I nod absently. It's so nice to have someone here to share this part of the day with. Normally I'd watch the news while I finished dinner or maybe read a few chapters of a book. But my mind is running in so many directions and I know that I won't be able to concentrate on anything with these questions unanswered.

"Eli and Kay came by yesterday. I think they're a little worried

191

about us spending so much time together. I guess Eli did background checks on all of you guys when Tank first found you."

The hunted look on his face makes me sad. That's not how I want to make him feel, like I'm judging him for his past choices. Especially since he's never judged me for mine.

"I guess I shouldn't be surprised. I've told you over and over again that I'm not a good guy, Sasha. I've done a lot of things that I regret."

"You think this makes a difference to me? I know you Gabe. I'm not judging you. I just want to understand."

Gabe's hand pauses in the middle of massaging the ball of my foot. After a heartbeat, the gentle motion starts again.

"Things were hard for our moms. Paula worked as a caretaker for an elderly cousin, which didn't pay much, and my mom was always a breath away from getting fired from her janitorial job. There never seemed to be enough money."

He looks so far away and when he pauses, I'm scared to even ask what happened next. Even though I know everything worked out for them in the end, it hurts my heart to think of Gabe and Zack watching this unfold as little kids. My comfortable upbringing shielded me from this kind of suffering and it's shocking to see it from the inside. And makes me more than a little ashamed that I've never thought about these kinds of things before.

He finally seems to come back to the present. "I don't want you to think things were all bad. We had a ball growing up. In case you couldn't tell, both of our moms are pretty gutsy ladies and they found ways to get by. Most of the time anyway."

"Most of the time?"

His fingers tighten on my ankle. "Zack got sick a lot. He always had a compromised immune system but we didn't know he was diabetic then. Doctors aren't cheap and the bills were just piling up. We were fourteen when we were evicted and had to live in our car for a while. I think our moms were terrified that we'd get split up and sent to different foster homes."

Suddenly it's like a light bulb comes on.

"That's when you started stealing cars, isn't it?"

My heart breaks right down the center when he nods silently.

A second later, his thumb strokes up the ball of my foot again. We stay just like that until the timer goes off and I have to get up to take the food out of the oven. Over dinner it seems like we've made a silent pact not to discuss it any further but I can feel him watching me when he thinks I'm not looking.

When I lead him down the hall to my bedroom later that night, it feels so natural, so right to take turns using my small bathroom to brush our teeth and get ready for bed. As Gabe climbs in the bed and pulls me back against him, it occurs to me that this is the first time we've shared a bed without making love.

But as his arm tightens around my waist and his breathing turns even and slow, it feels like love to me.

Chapter Thirteen

Gabe

Over the next few weeks, Sasha and I settle into a comfortable rhythm. Between her temp jobs, her regular gig at the Piedmont and her work getting the club ready, staying over during the week is the only way I get to see her. If anyone had told me a few months ago that I'd basically be cohabitating with a woman and liking it, I would have thought they'd inhaled too much exhaust. But I do like it.

Almost as much as I like Sasha.

I'm pulling up to the shop after meeting with a vendor when my phone rings. It's Luke. When I see his name on the screen I immediately take the call. He and Tank have been working together to get information on Blade. He's not the type for chitchat so if he's calling now, it means he has answers.

"Luke? What's up?"

"Gabe, I have you on a conference call with Tank. His boss was able to use his contacts within the FBI to get access to Interpol."

"Hey Tank. What have you guys found?"

Tank's deep voice rumbles across the line. "Eli was able to get some info on the names you guys sent. They're aliases for members of the Irish Mafia. Every single one of them."

"Fucking hell. If Max is on their shit list, then we're all in for it. I knew he wasn't telling me the truth."

"You asked him about it? What did he say?"

It seems so long ago now, that day when I barged in on Max demanding answers. Afterward, I was so hell-bent on getting to Sasha and making sure she was safe that I hadn't taken time to analyze our father's strange behavior. But now looking back, I can see that I should have put the pieces together. Max had been deeply shocked when I described Blade. He'd looked terrified.

"The only thing Max told me was to keep my loved ones close. Because men like that don't care who they hurt to get what they want. At the time I didn't pay much attention to his reaction but he was scared. Shitless."

Luke speaks up again. "Which means he knows why they're after him. He must have been in a lot of trouble back in the day for them to be coming after him now. I mean, dude is like a million years old and has a bad heart. He's not exactly a threat to anybody now, right?"

His comment, ridiculous as it is, makes me wonder. Luke has a point. Max has been living a life not unlike most wealthy older Americans. He stays at his luxury hotels drinking high-caliber scotch surrounded by a bevy of pretty assistants. How the hell did he run afoul of the Irish Mafia?

"Maybe he's got gambling debts or something. That's the only thing I can think of. Unless this really is some old vendetta coming back to bite him in the ass years later."

Tank snorts. "Whatever the case, his shit isn't our problem. Or it shouldn't be. I'm only concerned with making sure this doesn't affect us or our families. We need to take action."

"You mean go after him?" Luke sounds a little too excited by the idea.

"Hell no. I'm just saying we need to take precautions." Tank pauses. "Gabe, have you told Sasha about any of this?"

"Are you going to warn me away from her, too? Because Finn and Eli have already threatened to cut off all my appendages. You'll have to get in line."

They both laugh.

"No, I'm just saying that we need to keep our women safe. I'm thinking they all need protection. Emma has resisted so far but she's getting a bodyguard whether she wants one or not. I'm suggesting that you guys might want to do the same. Luke, I'm not sure if your mom will let you but if you need me to, I can recommend some older guys that could blend into the crowd at the bakery and she won't suspect a thing."

"Yeah, I appreciate it man."

It feels like things are escalating faster than I can keep up. Bodyguards and mafia members aside, I'm not sure how I'm going to keep Sasha away from all this but I know I have to try. I think of all the times when she's been working at her club. Alone.

Something dark and twisted awakens at the thought of her alone and vulnerable. No doubt she won't thank me for it but I'm willing to do whatever's necessary to keep her safe.

Even if it's not what she wants.

* * * * *

Over the next week things are quiet. I don't hear any more until Tank calls to tell me that Blade left town. Max seemed pretty sure that he could handle things so maybe Blade got what he wanted from him. Or maybe not. Either way, I'm just glad he's not our problem anymore.

I'm talking to a customer on a Friday morning when Sasha storms into the shop. The door slams shut behind her, the bell overhead ringing like crazy. By the look on her face, I don't have time to get her in private before she blows up.

"Gabe Marshall, I can't *believe* you!"

Arthur Winston looks up from the forms he's filling out and then takes a step to the side. "I've been married long enough to recognize the look of a woman on a mission. I'm getting out of the way."

We've been handling Arthur's vehicles for years now so I know he's familiar with our paperwork. "Just leave the form when you're done, Art. Zack will call you when it's ready."

I come around the counter and motion for Sasha to follow me to the back. She looks like she wants to say something but she follows

197

me until we get in the office. As soon as the door closes behind us, she whirls around.

"You hired a construction crew to finish the renovations at my club. Did you think I wouldn't find out?"

I was actually hoping she wouldn't find out until they were done. I should have known that she wouldn't be able to stay away, even on days when she's not scheduled to be there. The club is her dream.

"The thought of you working by yourself to get things ready makes me crazy. It's not safe at night and those locks are hardly secure."

"I guess you'd know that better than I would." She immediately covers her mouth. "I'm sorry. That was a low blow."

Her words settle right in the pit of my stomach like I've swallowed a rock. "Maybe but it's the truth. I do know better just how dangerous this world can be and I don't want you at risk. I have the money to hire a crew so I did it. And I would do it again if it means you're safer."

She throws her handbag down in the chair behind my desk.

"Damn it, Gabe. You knew that I wanted to do this myself! It's not about the money or even safety. I'm not an idiot. I don't stay too late so there are other people around and someone always knows where I am. But now that there's nothing for me to do it feels like it's not really my project anymore."

I pull her into my arms and rest my chin on top of her head. "I hate when you're angry with me."

She squeezes me around the waist. "I'm not doing it for kicks, Gabe. I told you that I wanted to accomplish this on my own. You knew my feelings about it and you just bulldozed right over them."

Now that some of her initial wrath has been expressed, I can see that she's frustrated. And hurt.

I tip up her chin gently, holding fast when she tries to turn her head away. "Sasha, I'm a wealthy man."

She starts to protest but I kiss her into silence. "Just let me say this. I'm a wealthy man. I never thought I would be but there it is. I haven't earned it. And I'm sure as hell not the kind of guy who deserves it so I need to use this money to help the people that I care about. If I can't do that I'll go crazy."

"Am I?" she asks in a small voice. Then she peeks up at me shyly. "Someone you care about?"

"More than you can ever know." I rest my forehead against hers. We stay like that for a few minutes, breathing in tandem. Finally she rests a hand lightly against my cheek.

"I care about you, too."

* * * * *

Once Sasha leaves, I drop down into the chair behind my desk. It's quiet up front so I figure most of the guys bailed when they heard Sasha on the warpath. She's got the entire crew wrapped around her little finger so if there's a fight between us, I'm already aware that they would all be firmly on her side.

My phone vibrates in my pocket and I answer it without looking at the screen. When I hear Cole's voice, I curse the impulsive action.

"Hey kid. You given any thought to that job I told you about?"

Despite my repeated refusals since the day he met me at that old warehouse, he seems to think that I'm playing hard to get. He's called multiple times and even come by the shop. That didn't go over too well. Jim knows that he was the one who got me into boosting cars in the first place so he wasn't too happy to see him show up here.

"I told you. I'm out of that life."

He grunts. "I really need you on this one. This is a big score. The kind that could really set me up, you know?"

He's never sounded quite this desperate before. The kind of desperation that comes from either debt or drugs. My head drops forward into my hands. Even though I know intellectually that I'm not responsible for anyone else's actions, I can't help feeling a pang of regret and sympathy for him. He got me into trouble, yes, but he also got me out of trouble at times, too. He was my friend.

"Hey, man. You know I can spot you the cash. Whatever you need."

My words introduce a new form of tension. Cole has always been a proud type and despite being a thief, he's always had an almost old-fashioned code of honor. He doesn't believe in charity.

As expected, he doesn't sound happy with my offer. "I didn't call for a handout. This is a job offer. I'm trying to give you a shot at it before we have to find someone else. I'm sure you don't want to be stuck in that shop fixing other people's fancy cars forever. Just think about it."

He hangs up and I'm left with a vague sense of unease and a cloying sense of guilt. So far I've been able to keep my financial windfall relatively quiet. Not too many people know and the only big thing I've bought so far is my house. It feels weird knowing that all my old friends are still struggling and I can only help them so much.

I look up to see Josie watching me from the doorway. She gives me a little smile. "There was a time when you wouldn't have been able to say no. You've become a better man right before my eyes."

I squeeze my temples between my palms. There's a knot of tension between my brows that makes me feel like my forehead is about to crack open. "Hah. I would be a better man if I didn't feel a little flash of excitement wondering what the job is."

Her eyes soften. "I said you were a better man, not a robot."

I smile in acknowledgment. Maybe there's a part of me that will always miss the excitement of my old life but that doesn't mean I'm doomed to repeat my mistakes. Especially when I have so many other things in my life that make staying on the straight and narrow worth it.

"You're still coming to my show tomorrow, right?" At my groan, Josie looks hurt. "It's okay if you forgot. You don't have to come."

"No, it's not that. I've had it on the calendar for weeks but that was before."

"Before Sasha?" she finishes.

"Yeah. I guess I'll have to see how she feels about spending a Saturday night looking at erotic photos. But even if she's not into it, I'm definitely coming. Zack is, too. You know we wouldn't let you down."

She nods. "I hope Sasha comes with you. If she's with you she's obviously not a complete prude."

I snort at the thought.

Josie turns to go but she pauses in the doorway. "It may not feel like you've come that far but you really have. A year ago, you would have been tempted to take the job despite the risks. I think you would have still said no, but you would have hesitated. There was no hesitation in your voice just now. I'm not sure if it's Sasha's influence but you've really changed."

She waves before she turns to leave. Her words give me hope, dragging me back from the depressive state that pulls at me when I think about Cole's situation. Under different circumstances, my life could have gone down that same path. But with Sasha, for the first time I truly have hope that I can forge an entirely different life. The kind of shiny, perfect life that I used to believe was reserved for only a select few. The lucky ones. With her it all seems possible.

I love her.

Maybe it's finally time to unclip the tethers of the past and move into the future with nothing holding me back.

But just as soon as the thought occurs to me, my dark side intercedes. I broke into the warehouse just because I wanted answers about Blade. I'd been all too happy to bend the boundaries of my new morality when it suited me.

I've changed but what if I haven't changed enough?

Chapter Fourteen

Sasha

When Gabe picks me up Saturday night, the appreciative look on his face makes the hours I spent getting ready worth it. The amethyst colored cocktail dress I'm wearing gives me a perfect hourglass shape and I've pulled my hair into a sassy side ponytail so the curls cascade over my mostly bare shoulder. I spent almost a month's rent on this dress and I've used every makeup trick I've learned over the years from performing.

That's what tonight feels like. A performance.

Ever since he told me about Josie's show, I've had to fight down my jealousy. I'm not the kind of girl that assumes the worst of other women and the way I feel about him being friends with Josie makes me feel petty. I want to be the cool type who is totally okay with her man having a gorgeous female friend but I can't deny that I feel the pressure to look perfect tonight.

I slip my arms into my long black coat and follow him out to the car. "So, where is this exhibit anyway?"

Gabe holds open the passenger side door for me. He doesn't answer until he rounds the car and gets in the driver's seat. "It's in a gallery in Norfolk. It's a very exclusive show highlighting new artists. The owner handpicks who will be in the show every year and since it's so exclusive, the artists usually sell out and receive commissions for future work, too."

Pride runs through his voice. I can tell he's really happy for her. He sounds the same way when he talks about Zack. It calms me somewhat. Maybe he really does think of her like a sister.

But that doesn't mean she feels the same way, a nasty little voice in the back of my head taunts.

Determined not to even go down that path, I focus on the music playing. Gabe usually listens to alternative music or hard rock but this time the radio is tuned to a jazz station. On the drive across the bridge to Norfolk, we listen in comfortable silence with Gabe occasionally asking me questions about the songs. Before long I'm telling him stories about listening to my father's old records and giving my first concerts with my family as the audience. It touches me that he's made such an effort to learn more about the kind of music that I like.

Gabe pulls into a parking garage and we walk through the structure and out onto the street. I drag my coat closer around me to block the wind. It's hard to walk fast on the skinny heels I chose to wear tonight and I'm damning my love of footwear when I finally see the sign for the exhibit. I stop mid-stride.

"Eroticism in art." I glance over at Gabe, who suddenly won't meet my eyes.

I cross my arms. "Funny how you didn't mention the type of show. Let's get it all out there. Josie is taking erotic photos and asks you to come to the show. Did she ask you to pose for the photos, Gabe? Is that what I'm walking into?"

He looks horrified. "No! There has never been anything between me and Josie. I've always been honest with you, Sasha. We're just friends."

I turn away before he can see the skeptical look on my face. I'm sure that he believes that because it's what he wants to believe. But anyone with eyes can see that Gabe is not the kind of guy you put in the friend zone.

Gabe takes me in his arms, pulling me against his chest. "If you want to go, then I'll take you home. I should have told you what kind of show it was. But I knew how it looked and I wasn't sure how you'd react. This is a big deal for her and I just want to support her. She doesn't get a lot of support from her family."

Now I really feel like a grinch. "We don't have to leave. I'm not trying to make you choose between us."

The arm around my waist tightens. "I hope you don't ever ask me to choose. Because with the way you make me feel, I'm afraid of some of the choices I'd make."

He looks suddenly uncomfortable with what he's just revealed. I'm just as confused. All the lines have been blurred between us from the beginning and even though we made rules, we never discussed what we'd do if either of us got in too deep.

Without another word, he grabs my hand and we walk into the gallery together. I surrender my coat at the door and take Gabe's arm. When I get my first glance at the crowd I'm doubly glad I splurged on a new dress. Most of the women are wearing formal attire and it feels like we're wading into a sea of diamonds and precious stones. I clasp the thin gold chain around my neck. Suddenly I feel underdressed.

"This way." Gabe leads me to the left side of the gallery. He stops in front of a sign with Josie's name on it. "This is her collection."

The photographs are arranged in a semi-circle. The first photo shows a woman looking over her shoulder at a couple passionately embracing. She has tears in her eyes. The next photo is a woman leaning toward a mirror touching up her lipstick. She's topless.

Nudity is definitely not something I'm super comfortable with coming from such a religious family. But the way it's presented makes her curves seem like just another feature, like her full lips or the mole on her cheek. It's classy. Despite my initial misgivings, I'm impressed.

"She's really talented."

And I'm not saying it because she's Gabe's friend. We stop in front of a picture of a couple spooning on a bed. The man is curved completely around his woman, cradling her in the shell of his body like he can protect her from the world. Josie took the shot from a lower angle so it feels like you're right there peering over the edge of the bed. Looking at the picture makes me feel a strange sort of awareness. It captures the way I think a lot of women wish they could feel after intimacy. Cherished.

Gabe is the only man I've ever been with who makes me feel that way.

"Yes, she is very talented." Gabe sounds a little shocked.

"Haven't you seen her work before?" Since he said they've been friends since high school, I would have assumed that he'd seen her work plenty of times. Unless she's really private about it. I understand that. Kay has been writing songs for a long time but it was years before she would even show me and I'm her best friend.

"I have. But not like this. She used to do regular portraits. Some landscapes. Even wedding photography. She always said that photographing people when they aren't posing is her favorite thing to do. But it was never like this. This is truly what she's meant to do."

Gabe turns at the sound of his name. Zack is waving him over to a group of people on the other side of the room.

He hesitates. "I wish I could stay here and hide with you. Unfortunately that man with Zack is one of our best customers. So I have to go play nice."

I push him away slightly. "Go and mingle. I'm going to see the rest of the exhibit."

"Are you sure? I didn't bring you here to abandon you, I promise."

I stand on tiptoe to kiss his cheek. "I'll be fine. I'm excited to see the rest of her pictures. Plus, I'd rather wander and explore than get stuck in conversation with people I don't know."

Most of the people here came with someone so it's surprisingly easy to wander without anyone bothering me. Since the focus is on the photographs, there's not much pressure to make conversation unless you want to. When I move to another cluster of photos, I realize that I've left Josie's display. I move from section to section, admiring the talent of the artists.

All of the photos focus on physical intimacy but each has a different tone. Some are sweet, some are raunchy and there are some that invoke a sense of violence that I find disturbing. Although they make me uncomfortable, I understand the artist's intentions. Sex brings out the basest emotions in all of us and I've had a few boyfriends whose love felt destructive rather than nurturing. It's not a good thing but it's reality.

By the time I circle the entire room and come back to Josie's collection, I have to admit that hers are my favorite.

"Sasha! I'm so glad you came." Josie appears at my elbow looking like a screen siren in a black sheath dress and pearls. Her dark hair contrasts with her dramatic red lip color in an elegant way.

"Hi. I was just admiring your photos again. Everyone here is really talented but yours are definitely the best."

Although I doubt my opinion matters that much to her, she beams at the compliment.

"Thank you. I've worked so hard on this series. I almost didn't participate in this show. It's such an honor to be asked but I wasn't sure I could deal with all the fallout. My parents still aren't speaking to me. I guess I should look at that as a positive thing."

There's nothing in her attitude or behavior that makes her seem insincere. She seems so nice. And charmingly self-deprecating. I instantly feel worse for the things I've been thinking about her.

"Well, I'm glad you decided to do it."

"I probably wouldn't have if Gabe hadn't talked me into it. He's always believed in me. Even when I didn't believe in myself. He's an amazing friend."

When she talks about Gabe her expression softens. It's clear that she loves him. Jealousy flares again, strong and bright. I don't want to ask but it'll always be between us otherwise.

"Is that all he is? A friend?"

Josie turns to me with sympathy in her eyes. "*Yes*. Gabe protected me at a time in my life when I was really vulnerable. But he's not the one…" She glances over her shoulder.

I follow her line of sight to where Zack stands. He's talking to Gabe and the man I assume is their customer. He's cleaned up for the event and is wearing a black suit, white shirt and a blue tie. He slicked up the front of his hair instead of doing his usual row of spikes.

His eyes drift over Gabe's shoulder and when he notices Josie looking, he stiffens. An intense look passes over his features before he turns his back. I look over at Josie. She looks tortured.

"*Oh*. I think I understand."

"Yeah. I just wanted to make sure you understood. I know most people don't. But I've never seen Gabe like this with a girl before. Don't give up on him when he gets weird. There are times when he gets really remote. Really distant. It can be work to get him to open up. But he's worth it."

When her gaze goes back to Zack, I actually feel a little sorry for her. I'm not sure what the deal is between them but she's obviously hurting. The picture of the woman watching the couple with tears in her eyes is starting to make a lot of sense.

I turn to Josie. "Would you mind showing me around? I've looked at the other collections but I'd love to see the ones you think are the best."

The night started with me thinking Josie was the enemy but we actually have more in common than I thought. We're both in love with men we're not sure how to reach.

As she leads me away, I hope that I can distract us both.

*   *   *   *   *

Josie shows me some of her favorite photos in the show and even introduces me to the owner of the gallery. He's the flirtatious type and I can't help giggling a little as he compliments my dress. He has a manner that reminds me of Gabe, playful and charming. He's an older man, tall and distinguished looking, who clearly thinks that

Josie walks on water.

I leave them discussing the possibility of another show and wander some more.

Gabe appears by my side while I'm examining one of the more raunchy photos. He raises an eyebrow. Despite my determination to be worldly and sophisticated, heat climbs my neck.

"Interesting. I didn't even know the human spine could bend that way." He takes my arm in his. I follow his lead and allow him to guide me in between the exhibits.

"Where are we going?" I don't see Zack anywhere and the crowd has started to thin. We're able to move through the room easily now.

"I want to show you something." Gabe's tone is clipped.

I glance over at him in trepidation. Is he angry with me for not mingling? For a brief moment I wonder if Josie told him what I asked about them being just friends, then I dismiss that idea. I saw the way she looked at Zack. She's definitely not after anyone else.

"Are you okay?" I ask softly. Gabe doesn't answer but suddenly turns right and pushes me through a door. The door shuts behind me and we're plunged into darkness. Then I feel his hands skim up my arms and into my hair.

"Gabe, where—"

My words are swallowed by the vehemence of his kiss. His hands grip my face so hard it almost hurts and I can barely breathe. When he pulls back, I suck in a few desperate breaths before he takes my mouth again, gentler this time. Desire sparks and I wrap one leg around his waist, using it as leverage to climb his body until I'm in his arms.

He grips my ass, supporting my weight. It feels like I'm caught in some kind of tornado as I run my hands all over him, trying to touch, taste and feel all at once.

"He was smiling at you," Gabe rasps. His mouth is on my ear and I shudder violently as he places hot, suctioning kisses all the way down my neck.

"Who? What?" I stammer as he angles me against the wall, using it to support some of my weight so he can get his hands free.

"Mr. Hartwell. The owner of the gallery."

I'm mindless at this point, not able to concentrate on anything other than his hands working my dress up around my waist.

"We were just talking. Josie introduced us."

His fingers finally reach their destination. He shoves my panties to the side and plunges two fingers deep. My pussy immediately clamps down and the invasion feels so good that I cry out. He covers my mouth with his, swallowing the rest of the sound.

"He was smiling at you. Looking at you. And I knew exactly what he was thinking. He wanted *this*. He wanted what's mine."

His fingers haven't slowed down this entire time, plunging, retreating and then plunging again. Tears gather at the corners of my eyes. The pleasure is so intense, more so because it's so sudden. Gabe is always so careful with me, spending time to slowly stoke my desire so that I'm desperate for it. But this is so raw, motivated by some dark emotion that's driving him to conquer and claim. He's claiming me and I love it.

"Shouldn't be doing this here," he mumbles. "But I need you to come. Need to feel it."

His thumb circles my clit, pressing in exactly the right spot to set me off. His fingers slam into me again and I shake uncontrollably as the orgasm rolls through me. We stay like that, gasping together, breathing in each other's air until he finally pulls his fingers free. The sudden sensation makes me shudder again. I tentatively swing my legs down and shimmy my skirt into place.

He leans down, his lips searching over my forehead and down my nose until he gives me a soft kiss. "I don't want you to go home tonight. I want you with me. Always. Move in with me."

My heart clenches. "Gabe, I can't do that."

"Why not? There's not enough hours in the day for me to see you, be with you. I always want more. I will always want more of you, Sasha. I'm in love with you."

It's almost like an emotional punch. His words uncork an endless fountain of joy inside me.

"I love you, too. So much."

He presses his forehead to mine. "Move in with me. I don't want to spend another night without you."

His words are convincing and I can feel my resolve wearing thin. But this is something that's too big to compromise on. I was willing to bend by keeping things casual because I knew Gabe wasn't ready for more than that. And I know that this is his way of trying to move forward. But living together without being married … I cringe thinking about what my parents would say. What they'd think.

I bury my face in his shoulder. I hate knowing that no matter what I decide, one of us will be hurt.

"I'll think about it," I promise. It seems to appease him because he gives me another soft kiss and then smoothes my hair back from my face. By the time he pulls open the door to the closet I feel like I'm presentable. On the outside at least.

Inside I'm a mess.

It's not just about how I feel about Gabe. Based on feelings alone, I would give him anything. But I don't know how long I could survive living with him under the strain of all that disapproval.

I have more in common with Josie than I thought.

One of the images from the exhibit comes to mind of a woman bent over backwards. I've bent a lot of my principles so far because I was sure that it would be worth the pain.

I'm just not sure how far I can bend before I break.

* * * * *

Curled up in my pajamas, I pull out a spiral notebook and start jotting down ideas. After all the sensuality of the art show, I'm determined to find ways to incorporate that into the club. Ever since my father told me his secret about the club, I've been researching it on the internet, hoping someone might have uploaded some old pictures of what it looked like.

I probably can't afford to make it look exactly like the old club but surely I can pull in a little sexy retro glamour. It would be so worth it just to see the look on my father's face. Part of me wishes I could find that charlatan who swindled him out of his money and force him to pay up. It makes me so angry that some criminal with no conscience stole my father's dream. I would love to be able to give a little piece of it back to him.

I write down all the things I think I can handle on one side of the paper and then all the stuff that I'm not sure about on the other. On the left I have entertainment and furniture. On the right I have taxes and payroll. Then I add insurance to the list. And marketing.

With a disgusted sound, I drop the pen. There are so many things that I have no idea about and all of those things are vital to starting a business. Maybe I shouldn't have been so quick to turn down Gabe's help. Even though I want to do this myself, he is really good at this kind of stuff. At times like these, I wish I had a partner. If Kay wasn't so busy recording and growing little mini-Eli's then I could ask her. I rest my head against the back of the couch.

When I wake, it's pitch black in the room. The television has a timer so it shuts off after a certain amount of inactivity. I stand in the dark room, padding in my bare feet back to my bedroom in the dark when I hear it. *Scritch scritch scritch.*

There it is again. A soft scratching sound. Then the loud click of the latch. Shock and fear race through me. Someone has just opened the back door.

I move backwards slowly, praying that none of the floorboards under my feet squeak and betray my position. All the times that Eli lectured me to set the alarm as soon as I get home run through my head. That always seemed so over the top so I usually set it right before I go to sleep. But now as I inch backward, praying that I can get to my room undetected, I curse my stubbornness. If I'd just listened to him then the silent alarm would have already alerted him that there was a problem.

I have to get to my room so I can call for help.

As soon as I cross the threshold to my room, I shut the door, turning the knob all the way so the latch doesn't catch and make noise. I turn the lock and then hurriedly rush to the bed. My laptop is sitting on top of the covers. I grab it and my phone from the nightstand, my heart racing so hard I can barely breathe. I carry everything into the closet and drop to the floor.

I dial 911 and then open my laptop. My hands fumble with the lid, fear making me clumsy. I'm typing a message to Kay in the messaging app when the emergency dispatcher answers. I whisper my address and that there's an intruder just as a message comes in from Kay.

- - *Eli is on the way. Stay where you are!*

I sit quietly, responding to the emergency dispatcher to tell her my location in the house. Suddenly there's the sound of glass breaking from out front.

"Whoever it is just broke something," I whisper. "They're making a lot of noise. I don't think they know I'm here. What if they try to come back here?"

"Ma'am, please stay calm. The police are en route." The dispatcher's calm, steady voice is only making me panic more.

There's some psycho in my house breaking stuff. And if they think they're in an empty house, what will they do when they finally realize they aren't alone?

Just then I hear the sound of my bedroom doorknob turning. It makes a clicking sound as whoever is on the other side tries to turn it again and again. There's a muffled curse and then a bang. I hang up on the operator, not wanting the intruder to hear the sound of her voice. I close the lid on my laptop and silence my phone. I shrink back deeper into the closet.

My hand bumps into something hard and pointy. I grope around until my fingers close around the shoe. I almost want to sob and laugh at the same time. I'm trapped in my room and the only weapon I have readily available is a high-heeled shoe.

I clutch the shoe tighter to my chest when I hear the sound of sirens in the distance. Then a few minutes later I hear someone call out, "*Police*! Anyone here?"

I'm shaking so badly I can't even answer. I crawl out of the closet and run to open the bedroom door.

"Is it safe to come out?"

The beam of a flashlight hits me in the face and I squint against the sudden light in the darkness. The officer lowers his weapon and his flashlight. "Yes, ma'am. You called about a prowler?"

"Someone was here. I heard them." I open the door wider and then gasp.

An ornately carved knife is embedded into the wood of my bedroom door. The blade goes directly through a picture.

Of me.

* * * * *

For the next half an hour, I have to recount the story of what happened and point out the damages. Nothing appears to have been taken but it's hard to tell since my living room has been trashed. The cushions on the couch have been slashed with a knife and all my vases have been shattered.

The picture of me is still on my bedroom door. I was told not to touch or move anything, not that I wanted to anyway. It gives me the creeps every time I look in that direction. I'm not sure what day it was taken but it must have been recently because I'm wearing my new down coat. In the picture I'm laughing, my face turned up to the sky. There are words written on the bottom but I only know because the officer told me what it said.

You take from me, I take from you.

Just remembering the words sends a chill up my spine, not that I have any idea what that means. I haven't taken anything from anyone. And I never have. I would never steal.

Eli arrives in the middle of everything and smoothly takes over. I'm grateful for his interference for once. When he sees my fingers shaking, he even uses my cell phone to call Gabe.

While he deals with the police, I sit on the couch clutching my phone in my hands. The next thing I know Gabe is kneeling before me. His dark eyes are awash with regret. I launch myself into his arms and cling to his neck.

"I knew I should have brought you home with me. Oh god, Sasha." His voice breaks and he suddenly grabs me in a hug so tight that my ribs ache. He hefts me in his arms and sits awkwardly on the couch with me in his lap.

"What happened?" he asks.

My tears have subsided a little at this point so I wipe my eyes and stand. I point to the back door. "He came in through that door. I was asleep on the couch. When I got up, I heard some strange sounds. Then I heard the door open. I barely made it to my room."

Eli appears at my elbow. "The police are about done. They're going to dust for prints and they're taking your neighbor's statement. She says she saw a guy hanging around earlier today. They're also going to analyze the photo and see if they can find out where it was printed."

"Photo?" Gabe raises his eyebrows.

Eli points to my bedroom door.

Gabe walks over and when he sees the note all the blood drains from his face. I'm stunned by the devastation in his eyes. Silently, he crosses the room and pulls me into his arms. I can feel his anguish.

"I'm okay, Gabe. I'm okay." I repeat the words, hoping if he hears it enough, he'll believe it.

He pushes back and the bleak despair on his face transforms into a determined look. He kisses me on the forehead again. "I have to go."

"Wait! Where are you going?" I follow him to the front door.

When he turns, something comes over his face and his

219

expression goes completely blank. I haven't seen this look on his face in so long that I forgot what it was like to have him look at me with no emotion in his eyes.

His mask is back and my Gabe is gone.

"Sasha, I was wrong when I told you that I could do this. This, all of this, is getting too real. You deserve the kind of guy that can be there for you, who can make you happy and hold you when you're sad. I tried to be that guy … "

It sounds like he's reading from a script. Despite that, my heart still drops to the floor. He's pushing me away.

"You do make me happy. I love you."

Gabe runs a hand through his hair in agitation. "That's because you don't really know me. I did more than just steal cars, Sasha. I stole lives. I manipulated people who trusted me. It's a compulsion I have to play with people. To see how far they'll let me go."

Everything he's saying is shredding me, like I'm swallowing knives. Listening to him, hearing his callous recitation of the things he's done is draining me until I have to cling to the doorframe just to stay on my feet.

"But I do know you, Gabe. That's not who you are. It's not." The words are as much for my benefit as his. I can't accept that he's not who I think he is. Because taking that away makes me feel like someone just died.

"I blame myself for this." His voice is smooth, almost seductive. And cold as ice. "You have to understand, someone like you is irresistible to someone like me. So naive, so trusting. It's like asking an alcoholic to stay away from the bar. You can try but if they build a bar near your house, you won't succeed. Playing with you was just too much temptation for me."

"I don't believe you. You're trying to push me away and it won't work. Just, please. *Talk to me.*" I've already lost my pride so I'm willing to beg. Anything to get him to stop saying these awful things.

Gabe makes a frustrated sound. "Your bank account number is 0004328567 and you keep the password written in an old day planner at the back of your closet."

I gasp but he's not done.

"Your social security card and birth certificate are tucked into that old Bible on your bookshelf. Probably so you don't forget where they are, am I right? Your mother's maiden name is Dalton. You told me that when you were telling me about your family. It was so easy to get everything I needed from you."

I'm crying so hard now that Eli has ditched any appearance of giving us space.

"What the hell is going on?" Eli growls, glaring at Gabe. He pulls me into his arms, putting himself between us.

"I'm telling Sasha the truth. That I'm not good for her. And if you care about her like I think you do, you'll make sure she doesn't follow me."

Then Gabe turns and walks down the driveway. I watch, feeling like everything I know has just gone up in flames.

Chapter Fifteen

Gabe

I want blood.

Walking away from Sasha's door, her soft cries ringing in my ears, feels like cutting off my own arm. Lying to her about how I feel took all the acting skill I have. It was torture crushing her spirit and it did just as much damage to me convincing her that everything she felt for me was a lie. I feel torn open and gutted.

But the gaping hole in the center of my chest is soon filled with boiling rage and one purpose.

Getting to Blade.

I want to hit him where he lives. This asshole was in Sasha's house. He could have done anything and I wouldn't have been there to help her. The enormity of just how vulnerable she is sends a paralyzing wave of fear through me.

I almost collide with someone coming up the driveway. Tank. I have to suppress a growl of impatience. Convincing Eli and Sasha that I'm an asshole was easy. It'll be harder to get by Tank. He's not easy to manipulate.

"Where are you going?" He stops squarely in my path knowing that I'll have to stop. If I want to get by him, I'd have to be able to push him out of the way. There are not many people big enough to take him.

"I have to go."

He doesn't move. "What do you mean you have to go? Sasha needs you right now."

"We broke up. She's not my problem anymore." I give up on moving him and just walk around him.

He grabs my arm and I shrug it off angrily. I'm too primed to be polite right now.

"You expect me to believe that Sasha's in danger and that you don't care?" Tank narrows his eyes. "I don't believe it. So I'll ask you again. Where are you going?"

Now this I don't need. If Tank thinks I'm going after Blade he'll try to stop me. And Sasha isn't safe with him out there.

"Just because we share DNA doesn't mean I owe you any explanations. I don't care what you believe as long as you get the fuck out of my way."

Tank finally takes a step back. "I don't know what the hell is going on but Gabe … " He eyes me with a hard look. *"Don't do anything stupid."*

I start walking down Sasha's driveway and then into the street. Direction won't matter. Blade will still be nearby. Watching. Waiting. Sure enough, after I walk two blocks over, I see him. He's got a baseball cap on but I know that walk.

"Hey!"

He looks back and then takes off running. I sprint after him, dodging around a parked car to follow him down a side street. As soon as I turn the corner, a fist plows into my stomach.

"Shit!" I swing out blindly, catching him in the arm.

He pulls me up and then unleashes a flurry of jabs to my chest. I manage to block a few and deliver a punch to his jaw that makes his head snap back but that doesn't slow him at all. It's clear that he's an experienced fighter and before long, he catches me on the side of the head so hard I see stars. Then his arms slashes out and fire explodes in my side.

He shoves me away and I stumble and land on one knee. Gravel and rocks tear at my jeans, sending little shards of pain to the skin. When I look up, there's a knife in his hand. I can't tell in the dark but I'm willing to bet it's the same kind of knife rammed into Sasha's bedroom door. Just the thought of it enrages me all over again. He sees the anger in my eyes and laughs.

This is where it ends, I think. Because with the look in his eyes I know that he will have no problem cutting my throat.

"I'm not going to kill you. Unless you force me to." He has a thick Irish accent. Tank's intel was good then.

"That knife isn't just for show," I remark. "Clearly you have no problem using it, either."

"Your last name is the only thing that saved you, *boyo*. That message was a warning. Most people don't even get one."

"My last name?" I pant, holding a hand to my aching ribs. When I pull my hand away, it's stained with blood.

Fuck.

"I had to come, to see what could make a man turn his back on his family, his country and his duty. This isn't how I wanted things to go but you brought this on yourself when you stole from me. I saw you at the warehouse."

His ramblings make no sense but all I care about is clarifying the last point. "I didn't take *anything* from you."

"Not at first. But you sent back your little friend. The redhead. He took something from me and I need it back."

"I didn't know." Damn Cole and his sticky fingers. "I'll get it back. Just leave Sasha alone!" Pain flares anew from the exertion of yelling and I struggle to calm down. Deep breaths cause a firestorm in my chest. I keep my hand pressed to my side as hard as I can.

"Get me my ring back and we'll see." His accent thickens as he points the knife at me.

"And you'll leave her out of this?"

He doesn't answer, just smiles that creepy smile. Then he's moving toward me.

"What do you mean about my last name?" I ask desperately.

He flips the knife, the blade glinting in the moonlight like a shooting star, before he catches it. "It's the same as mine."

I never even saw the punch coming.

* * * * *

When I wake up, the only thing I feel is pain. I can't even cry out. It would take energy I don't have to even make a sound so I just lie in agony hoping that someone will come along and put me out of my misery. Until I hear Tank's voice. Then I think, *anyone but him*.

I'm never going to hear the end of this.

Tank kneels next to me. "I told you not to do anything stupid."

He slips an arm under my shoulders and then hoists me up. My voice returns then, either that or the pain needs an outlet.

"That fucker hits like a freight train. I think his knuckles are made out of titanium."

Tank glances over at me, walking slowly so I can lean on him. "Looks that way. You haven't seen what your face looks like yet. What the hell were you thinking?"

"I had to, Tank. He can't hurt Sasha. I can't let that happen."

"Sasha is fine. Eli took her to his house. I'm more concerned about you right now. We need to get you to the hospital."

I scoff. "I don't need to go to the hospital. I've been beat up before."

We're almost to the end of the street now where Tank's SUV waits idling at the curb.

"Are you going to be able to get in by yourself or do you need me to help you? Maybe to fasten you into your car seat and give you a bottle, too?" Tank chuckles.

"You're enjoying this way too much. And the only bottle I need has Johnnie Walker on the label."

When he's helping me in the car he lets out a curse. "You were stabbed? *Jesus.*"

That's when I pass out for the second time.

Over the next few days things are a blur. There's a lot of noise and voices and then I'm floating on a blissful wave. Fluorescent lights overhead, antiseptic smell all around. That can only mean one thing. I wake briefly to a nurse adjusting my IV line and whatever she gives me knocks me out again.

When I wake again, I hear Zack's voice. *"Shouldn't he have woken up by now?"*

Someone answers, a soft feminine voice I don't recognize. I open my eyes and then immediately squeeze them shut when the bright lights in the room send a sharp pain through my head.

I glance over at Tank. "I guess the hospital was a good call."

He lets out a little laugh, relief in his eyes. "Surgery went well. The knife missed the important stuff. That's the good news. The bad news is that the police haven't caught the mugger who did this to you." His eyes narrow and then lift to something on the other side of me.

I turn my head to see a young woman with light brown hair and glasses observing us. She's wearing a white coat so I assume she's the doctor. It's confirmed when she pulls out one of those annoying little penlights that all doctors seem to have and shines it right in my eyes.

"A mugger. Right. How long have I been here?"

She moves the light back and forth. "It's been four days. Do you know where you are?"

"I didn't get hit that hard. Seven times twelve is eighty-four, my birthday is June 17 and ESPN is on channel 561. Can I go home now?"

The doctor frowns. "Mr. Marshall, we need to be sure that you don't have any complications."

"Just give me some good drugs and I'll be fine. I don't like hospitals."

Zack meets my eyes and there's a sad understanding there. We spent so much time with doctors when he was a child so I'm sure it's not easy for him to be here.

She finally puts the penlight away. "If you check out it will be against medical advisement." At my nod, she sighs. "I'll have the nurses prepare your discharge papers."

As soon as she's gone, I turn back to Tank. "I broke into the place where Blade was staying about a month ago. My friend Cole was with me. Apparently he went back and stole something from Blade. He wants it back. That's what this is all about."

Zack's face is stony when he says, "We'll take care of it. I'll make sure Tank knows where to find him." By the look on his face he's going to enjoy letting Tank scare the crap out of Cole. After this stunt I'm not defending him anymore. Old friend or not, his actions put us all in danger.

It takes a while for the nurses to get my discharge papers together so it's almost noon before we can leave. Getting home is a long process that requires a stop at the pharmacy for prescription painkillers and the complete loss of my pride when Tank has to carry me upstairs. Thank god Zack didn't tell our moms that I was coming home today. I remember bits and pieces of them at the hospital while I was so out of it. I can't deal with anything else right now. Right now, I need sleep.

I take the pills and slide under the covers. My hand brushes something soft and I hold up one of Sasha's hair ties. She uses them whenever she sleeps over to put her hair up in this ridiculously high ponytail that she calls "the pineapple." I was never sure what fruit had to do with anything but I've gotten used to her strange nighttime rituals and having her soft body next to mine. I've gotten used to loving her, my sweet silly girl.

Squeezing the fabric between my fingers, I slip into the reprieve of sleep. Sasha's face is the last thing on my mind.

*　*　*　*　*

The next morning, I feel worse, if that's possible. Every inch of my torso aches like a bad tooth and I'm pretty sure the painkillers are making me hallucinate. When I ask Zack why there's a frog eating my toast, he just laughs and gives me another pill.

I sleep until Zack shakes me awake again.

"What is it?" I mumble.

"You need to come downstairs. We have a visitor."

I'm too weak to dress myself so Zack helps me get a pair of sweatpants on and forces a T-shirt over my head. Getting down the stairs is just as difficult but I draw the line at anyone carrying me again.

Once we enter the living room, I stop. Max sits on the couch, his assistant Carole next to him. Luke, Tank and Finn are here, too.

When he sees me, Max's lip quivers. His hand comes up to cover his mouth. "This is what my lies have done. I had to see."

Zack helps me sit on the couch and I let out a deep sigh when I sink into the cushions. I know my appearance is shocking. One of my eyes is almost swollen shut and the bruise has already started to turn interesting shades of purple.

"What are you doing here, Max?"

He struggles to gain control of his emotions. Tears shine in his eyes as he answers. "To right a wrong. You asked me about Blade and I wouldn't tell you. Maybe if I had, I could have prevented this."

As angry as I've been at him since he came back into my life, I don't want him to bear the weight of this alone. "It probably wouldn't have stopped me. But he's a threat to someone I love so I'm asking you again. Will you tell us about him?"

Max contemplates us all before nodding slowly. Finn takes a seat on the couch next to me, stretching his leg out in front of him. Zack perches on the arm of the couch while Luke and Tank remain standing. Once he sees that he has our attention, Max starts talking.

"I came to this country without a shilling to my name. It was 1985." Shockingly his voice sounds completely different, the flat, generic American accent giving way to a lyrical, rolling brogue. We all look at each other in confusion for a moment.

"Wait a minute ... You're Irish?" Luke blurts.

Max chuckles, toying with the head of his cane. "So are you, young fella."

That gets a startled laugh from Luke. The tension in the room goes down slightly. For a moment Max looks younger, his face animated with pride as he looks around at all of us. Finally he takes another deep breath and continues.

"I was born in Belfast. My family seemed normal enough. My father had extremely strong political opinions, especially about Ireland's independence. But throughout my youth, I was unaware of just how strong his opinions were until I was older. He was the founder of a secretive group called Le Fírinne' that plotted to overthrow British rule. The name means *the truth*. It started as a political group with high ideals but by the time I was an adult it had become something else. Something much more dangerous."

"Like the IRA?" Luke asks.

Max nods. "I was groomed in all aspects of running the organization and soon was traveling around the world to foster connections that would help us get the supplies we needed. Arms, explosives, drugs ... " He makes a disgusted face. "My brother handled things at home while I was gone. I was the charming one so they trusted me to get what they needed." Max glances over at me.

231

I shift uncomfortably under his scrutiny. We're definitely two sides of the same coin, Max and I. It makes me feel an unexpected pang of sympathy for him. Suddenly something that Blade said comes back to me.

"Wait. Blade said that my last name is what saved me. Then he said that it's because my last name is the same as his. Is he our brother?"

Max shakes his head sadly. "No, although that's not the entire truth. My brother Donaghal had four sons. The oldest, Padraig, became the man you know as Blade. For me, marrying in Ireland was out of the question. Any children I had there would be squarely under the family's control. So I remained unmarried for years and helped raise my nephews as if they were my own. In many ways, I am responsible for him."

Anger flares. "Then why the hell is he trying to kill me?"

Guilt swims in Max's eyes. "The family considers everything that we own to be for the family's use. While I was traveling abroad, I began to dream of making money legally. They trusted me so I knew if I took some money, they wouldn't notice. At least not right away. I started building my business interests then and putting money aside that they couldn't touch. Then while I was in the States on business, I met Claire."

His eyes soften. Tank shifts and I can feel the tension coming from him. Finn has been staring down at his hands this whole time and he doesn't look up.

"You married her and stayed here for years. I don't get it. Why did you go back?" Tank sounds like he's trying to keep his anger under control.

Max glances over at me again. "Because I came home one day to find Donaghal sitting at the kitchen table. He had found out about my little secret and come to see for himself. Claire had no idea how much danger she was in. She was so trusting."

"She didn't know who he was?" Tank asks.

"I'd told her that I had a brother. She was thrilled to meet some of my family." Max looks so far away, his eyes dim with memories and regret. "I still marvel to this day that he left her alive. I think perhaps my brother might have still had a conscience at that point."

"So you ran away?" I'm suddenly seeing the incident with Sasha in a whole new light. His family had him backed into a corner and he'd responded with fear the same way I did. I imagine what it would have been like if I'd come to Sasha's house and found Blade there talking to her. My fingers clench into a fist.

"So I left," Max confirms. "The family didn't care that I was leaving children behind. As long as I came back and fulfilled my duty, they wouldn't concern themselves with some fatherless children halfway around the world. And I saw my opportunity to leave something of myself in the world that wouldn't be tainted."

He stops then, tears shining in his eyes. It's hard to watch. Years of regret and pain are etched in the lines of his face. Finally he collects himself and clears his throat.

"It was selfish but I wanted to spread my seed. I only chose strong women. I knew they could handle things on their own and would give my children all the love I couldn't. I told myself that I wouldn't come back. I broke that promise a few times but for the most part I stayed away. It was the best thing I could do for you. I'd already helped raise four killers. I had to do something to balance that out. I needed to bring some good in the world. And I did."

"So that's why you never came back." Finn finally speaks up.

Max nods. "I wanted you to hate me. I still do. Because as long as you hate me then you'll never end up like me. Each and every one of you is so extraordinary. You're everything I couldn't be."

"So why come back now? Is it because of Blade? Did he threaten you?" Luke demands.

"No, I came back because I wanted to see you before it was too late. I'm old. Control of Le Fírinne' long ago passed to the next generation but they still expected financial support, especially since they consider every dollar I've earned 'their' money. When they found out that I was starting to distribute my estate... Well, I knew there would be fallout. I just needed to see you first. Once the money is gone, it's out of their reach forever. I can't undo my past but I can give you all the chance to do something better."

Silence descends. I glance around at my brothers. None of us seems to have any idea what to do with this new information. Then as usual, Luke sums it all up.

"So, basically you stole from the Irish Mafia?" Luke whistles.

"*Fantastic.*" Tank drops his head back against the wall.

Max stands shakily. "My time is almost up and it's time to pay the piper. But before I'm gone I can set a few things right."

He goes pale and Carole rushes forward to help him back into his wheelchair. He pats her cheek affectionately. "Lads, it's time for me to be off."

He allows her to arrange a blanket over his lap and the two men who always travel with them appear in the doorway. They must have been in the kitchen this entire time.

Tank follows them out. When he returns he crosses his arms and looks at each one of us in turn.

"Okay, what the hell are we going to do?"

Chapter Sixteen

Sasha

I will forever be grateful that Eli was with me when my entire world fell apart. Gabe walked away without looking back once and it took me more than a minute to process that he wasn't going to turn around and come back.

When he disappears from sight, an anguished sound, one I didn't even know my vocal cords could produce, emerges from my throat. It's a mournful sound like a wounded animal. Eli holds me up and lets me cry on his shoulder until I'm drained and weak.

Afterward, Eli deposits me on the couch while he packs a bag.

And I don't argue. All I want is to curl up and sleep and there's no way I can sleep here after what happened. I make sure he brings my laptop and enough clothes to last for a week.

Luckily I know without even asking that Kay and Eli won't mind if I stay with them for a while. My living room looks like it's been through a food processor. Until I can order new furniture, there's no point in going back to my place.

I'm in a state of shock the entire drive to Eli's house. Even though it's the middle of the night, Kay must have been watching from the window because as soon as we pull into the driveway, she comes out of the house. Just the sight of her unravels the tenuous thread around my emotions. I lose it all over again. Kaylee is a born nurturer so she holds me and rocks me back and forth while I bawl like a baby. She takes me straight upstairs and I crawl in bed and cry myself to sleep.

When I wake up again early morning light fills the room. To my surprise Kay is on the other side of the bed. That makes me feel both grateful and pathetic.

"Kay, you didn't have to stay with me. I'm sure Eli wasn't happy sleeping alone."

"Eli is a big boy. He'll be just fine. You on the other hand, are not. I heard you crying in your sleep. I'm so sorry this happened to you."

Tears start anew at the thought. I'm not just crying because someone violated my home but because all I really want is Gabe. I let my guard down and trusted someone for the first time in a long time.

237

But he's not at all the person I thought he was. All I can do is mourn the loss of the love I thought was real.

Kay looks stricken as I wipe my cheeks.

"Oh sweetie. That day when we came to tell you about Gabe, you seemed like you knew everything."

I smile through my tears. "I thought I did. But I just thought he stole cars. I didn't know he was like the man who scammed my father. People like that steal so much more than money. They steal your dreams. And your ability to ever trust anyone again. He was just playing me the whole time. Like it was a game and he was just amusing himself by seeing how naive I could be."

She reaches across and grabs my hand. We used to sleep like this when we were little girls and spent the night at each other's houses. I was afraid of the dark for an embarrassingly long time but Kay never made fun of me for needing the nightlight. She was my comfort then.

I feel so lucky that she's still here to comfort me now.

"Come on. You slept through breakfast and I didn't want to wake you. But you need to eat something."

She coaxes me to the kitchen and then makes me soup and a grilled cheese sandwich. I didn't think I was that hungry but before long I'm devouring my food. A warm sense of comfort rolls through me. After lunch we curl up on the couch and watch some television.

Eli comes in at some point, watching me with a worried look. I force a smile to let him know that I'm okay. Although I'm pretty sure I won't be okay for a while. I thought I'd found someone that understood me and appreciated all that I am. Finding out that wasn't real was a greater blow than I could have imagined.

I've gotten over humiliation and failure many times before but this feels like drowning.

* * * * *

The next few days are more of the same. Kay has several recording sessions and I force her to go so she can't hover over me the whole time. It's a little better when I'm alone. I listen to music and read some of the books on my e-reader that I haven't had time to get to before. Keeping myself busy gives me a break from thinking too hard. But nothing helps me at night. All the distractions in the world don't keep the dreams away.

It's a week later when I've finally had enough. When I wake up I immediately push the covers back. I still have the desire to cry but I shove it down deep. Maybe it's because I've spent so much of the last few months wallowing in humiliation but I am over it.

I am stronger than this.

Gabe lied and that hurts but the things I've learned about myself aren't dependent on how I feel about him. I *am* smart and I *do* have good ideas. My greatest strength is my willingness to laugh at myself and make the best of whatever situation I'm in. So that's what I'm going to do.

When I enter the kitchen, Kay and Eli are sitting around the breakfast table.

"Morning." I sit and try to ignore their shocked looks.

I've been alternately weepy and depressed for the last week so

239

I'm sure my sudden chipper mood is a little strange. Eli watches me closely like he's afraid I'm going to start sobbing at any moment.

"Good morning. Here, I know how much you love pancakes." Kay brings me a plate with pancakes and bacon. The smell surrounds me and my stomach growls. I drown the stack on my plate with syrup.

"This is great." I glance over at Eli. "You get to eat like this every day? You are so lucky."

Eli just hums and then shovels another forkful of pancake in his mouth. Since Eli has a stack on his plate that's twice as big as mine, I know he agrees. No one cooks like Kay.

Kay sits across from us and snags a piece of bacon off the plate in the middle of the table. "Breakfast is the most important meal. And I think we can all use a little pick me up right about now."

Kay and Eli talk about random things but my mind isn't on any of it. After we clean up the table from breakfast, I take a quick shower and try to make my hair look presentable. I glance over at my cell phone. No calls. No texts. Nothing. I put my phone in my pocket.

No wallowing allowed.

I really want to climb back beneath the covers but I know if I do that, Kay will feel like she has to check on me all day. She's pregnant and doesn't need the added stress of worrying about me.

I grab my laptop and headphones. My plan for the day is to be lazy and binge watch some shows on Netflix. When I walk downstairs, Kay is sitting on the couch reading a magazine. Hope is playing with a set of alphabet blocks on the floor. I kneel down next to her and kiss her chubby little cheek. Looking at her reminds me of that conversation I had with Kay before all this started. My goal was to find my strength. It was about more than just owning something and proving to my family that I'm more than just a pretty face. It was about taking control. Ever since I went on that stupid show, I've allowed others to control how I see myself. As a failure. As a laughingstock.

Well, no more.

When I worked with Jackson on a song a few months ago, I knew even then that he was doing it mainly as a favor to Kay. They'd even let me sing at her local album release party. As much as I'd appreciated that, in hindsight the best part was helping Jackson create the song. I'd learned a lot from him about production and mixing. He'd shown me that the smallest changes in the editing process could completely change the sound of a song and influence the way it was received.

I open my laptop and put on my headphones. For the first time in months, I navigate to Youtube and pull up the video.

THE VIDEO. The bane of my existence and the one thing my family and friends know they aren't allowed to talk about.

I glance over at Kay quickly but she's absorbed in something on her e-reader so I tentatively press play. I'm braced to feel the same sense of humiliation as the first time I'd realized my audition was out there for all to see and make fun of.

I watch on the screen as I walk onstage. Oh god, I still remember how it had seemed like an endless number of faces in the audience.

The first judge, an older man with a head of shocking white hair speaks first.

"State your name."

"Sasha Whitman."

"And what are you going to sing for us today?"

"I'm going to sing 'Falling Hard' produced by Jackson Alexander."

The camera pans to the judges who all have the same pasted on smiles. As the music starts onscreen, I swallow a tickle of panic. This was when Chaz's last words to me had started running through my mind. He'd accused me of being delusional, of not caring about anything other than this contest. Which he'd considered laughable since, according to him, I had no chance to win. As it turns out he was right.

Tears cloud my eyes as I watch on the screen for the moment when I stop singing mid-verse. The judges are watching me with confused expressions. It had shocked me, too. In years of performing I've never forgotten the words to a song. The onscreen version of me opens her mouth over and over and then turns and bolts from the stage.

That's when it happens.

I trip and end up sprawled over a speaker, my skirt flipping up to reveal my yellow polka-dot panties.

The audience gasps and then all you hear are cheers, wolf whistles and laughter. I stop the video, the image of me with my ass on display frozen on the screen. This one picture has tormented me for months. It's been turned into online memes and endlessly mocked. The fact that my song was called "Falling Hard" and I then literally tripped and fell was an endless source of amusement for people. One moment changed the course of my life and turned me into a national laughingstock.

Anger rises and for once I don't stifle it or try to calm down. I have every right to be upset and I can't go through life pretending this didn't happen. I flash back to Gabe holding my hand the first time I showed him the club. Telling me I'm smart and that I have great ideas.

Nothing keeps you down for long, does it?

Whatever else he did, Gabe helped me see what makes me special. I don't allow things to keep me down and this should be no different.

I pull up the music software on my computer. Jackson encouraged me to work on some remixes for Falling Hard but after what happened, I never finished them. Producing was a totally different skill set and I hadn't had confidence in my work then. But things are different now.

A slow smile spreads across my face.

* * * * *

Later that evening, Eli comes in and drops his coat on the back of the couch. He looks exhausted.

Kay looks over her shoulder. "Hey, where have you been?"

Eli hesitates and glances over at me. There's obviously something going on and I can take a hint.

I close the lid of my laptop. "You guys talk. I can go upstairs."

Eli holds up a hand. "No, Sasha wait. You should hear this."

I sit slowly. Kay glances over at me with a worried look.

Eli sits and then rests his elbows on his knees. "There's something I have to tell you. About Gabe."

"Gabe is an asshole." I stand again. It's not surprising that Eli would go and track Gabe down after what he did to me. He's the type who takes chivalry seriously. But I don't want him apologizing for Gabe's foolishness.

"I think he said all that stuff to keep you away from him. That photo was some kind of message for him. I think he was worried for you. And he should have been." Eli looks down at his hands and then finally back up at me again. "Maybe you should sit down, Sasha."

The soft cadence of his voice fills me with dread. Gentle doesn't come naturally to Eli so the way he's looking at me and talking to me seems even more jarring. "What happened?"

"Gabe was stabbed that night after he left your house. Tank took him to the hospital."

I sit then, my breath forced from my chest when I hit the cushions so suddenly. "Oh my god. Is he okay? He's not ... " Was that why Eli looked so scared to tell me? Because Gabe is dead?

"No, he's okay. He had surgery but he's out of the hospital now. Apparently he checked himself out against his doctor's advice."

"I have to go see him."

Eli looks uncomfortable. "I'm not so sure that's a good idea. He asked me to keep you away from him. That must mean he thinks being around him is dangerous."

"I need to see him. Otherwise, you know I'll just break away at the first opportunity. Isn't it safer for me to go when you're right there?"

He doesn't look happy about it but he agrees.

We're all quiet in the car on the way there. I want to call Gabe but part of me thinks that just showing up is better. If he really pushed me away for my own good, then he isn't going to want me to come now. But I need to know that he's okay and I won't believe it until I see it with my own eyes.

Zack answers the door and immediately pulls me into a hug. Relief floods through me. He seems happy so I figure Gabe can't be hurt too badly. Josie peers around the corner from the kitchen and waves. I wave back and then turn to Kay and Eli.

As usual, Kay knows what I'm thinking.

"Go on. Don't worry about us. Take all the time you need."

I let out a deep breath and then with another encouraging nod from Zack, I climb the stairs. I push open Gabe's door and walk into the dim interior of his room. At the first sight of him, I can't help it. I gasp out loud.

His eyes pop open. The one that's all purple and swollen only opens halfway. "I must be in heaven or somewhere like it."

It's such a Gabe thing to say. Even when he's in pain he's trying to charm me.

"Haven't you learned by now pickup lines don't work on me?" I sink down next to him and push his hair off his forehead gently. I'm scared to even touch him. Every inch of his skin looks bruised and he has a huge bandage on the left side of his torso.

"My angel. It's not a line if it's the truth," he whispers.

Then he seems to wake from his half dream state. His hand grabs mine. "Sasha? You're here. You're really here."

"I am. I had to see you. Even if you lied to me I had to know that you're okay."

"No, you can't be here. It's not safe. Zack! Zack!" He yells over and over until his brother appears in the doorway. "You have to get her out of here. Keep her safe."

I shake my head. "I remember you telling me once that I was stuck with you until I was well enough to kick you out. Well, it's your turn now. I'm not going anywhere."

Zack smiles at us both. "It looks like you're in good hands. Sasha, his pain pills are on the nightstand. He's due for another dose in about an hour."

Gabe looks mutinous. After Zack leaves, I touch his hand lightly. "Is it really that hard to have me here?"

He turns toward me, the agony the movement causes him evident when he grimaces halfway through. "It's hard for me every day that I wake up and you're not with me. But I want you safe more than anything else."

His words stoke a renewed hope within me. "But you said … "

"I lied, Sasha. I'm a liar. A very skilled one. Convincing you that I didn't love you was the greatest con of my career. It ripped my heart out but when I saw that knife, I knew I had to do it."

I remember the picture and its ominous message. Eli had said that he thought Gabe was trying to protect me. Suddenly his cruel words and abrupt departure make a lot of sense. And the love I've been trying to stifle comes roaring back.

"Well, you aren't getting rid of me that easily." I rest my head on the only part of his body that isn't bruised, his shoulder. As I cry softly in happiness and relief, I feel him kiss the top of my hair gently.

"I love you so much, Sasha."

After a few minutes, I remember that Kay and Eli are still downstairs waiting for me. "Hold on. I'll be right back."

He nods drowsily. I walk back downstairs. Josie and Zack have disappeared. Kay and Eli are sitting in the living room holding hands. They both jump up when I appear.

"I'm going to be staying here for a little while. I'll get my stuff later but for now, yeah. I'll be here." I can tell I'm beaming when I say it.

"Are you sure you're going to be okay?" Eli looks so worried that all I can do is give him a hug. The big lug has really grown on me lately.

"I'm sure. I know what I want now."

"Oh honey, I'm so happy for you." Kay holds out her arms and hugs me close. When she pulls away, we're both wiping away tears.

Eli pulls Kay into his arms. "Come on, baby. Let Sasha take care of Gabe so I can take care of you."

I give Eli a grateful smile and walk them to the front door. He turns at the last second. "Sasha? The love of a good woman can overcome a troubled past. I'm proof of that." Then they're gone.

Upstairs, Gabe stirs when I come back in the room. I can tell he's been medicated because his eyes are slightly unfocused and he seems to have trouble following my movements around the room. I had started leaving random things at his house anyway so I pull out a pair of sweatpants and a T-shirt and change my clothes. Then I climb carefully into the bed next to him.

"I'm so sorry. So sorry, beautiful girl."

"Shh, it's okay." I hold a finger to his lips to stop the stream of apologetic words.

I'm just so grateful, so incredibly grateful that he's still here. That we get to have these moments. If things had ended differently, he could have been taken from me and I would have never known why. Worse, I would have lived the rest of my life thinking his cruel last words to me were the truth.

He turns his head and it hurts me to see what the effort costs him.

"I know you don't like the idea of just living together. You're a good girl." He smiles. "And I love that about you. So let's get married."

The hand that's stroking his hair freezes. Then my eyes fall on the medication bottle on his nightstand. Understanding dawns and I can't resist kissing the tip of his nose. He's so damn cute.

"Gabe, I think your medication is making you loopy."

He reaches up and grabs my hand. The gravity in his eyes makes me pause. He doesn't look delirious. But he has to be.

"I'm not dreaming and I'm completely serious. I am in love with you. And I don't ever want us to be apart."

Even though my heart sings, I know that a decision made in the spur of the moment isn't the best way to start a lifelong commitment. "I'll tell you what. If you still remember this conversation in the morning, then we'll do it."

He chuckles and then falls quiet. As his breathing evens out, I wonder if he'll remember this conversation tomorrow and be embarrassed. Just when I'm sure he's asleep, he opens his eyes again.

"Sasha? I want to tell you something."

"You can tell me anything."

He hesitates, as if he's afraid of how I'll take what he's about to say. "I was always a good liar. A master of manipulation. I didn't need to take people's money because if you know what you're doing, you can make them think it's their idea to give it to you."

"I have to admit, I still don't quite understand it. You have a good heart. I know you do." Even though he's changed, he still carries this negative view of himself. But I've seen the way he treats people. The way he cares for his family. For me.

"That's the most important part of a con. It's the appearance of being harmless. People always think they need to fear the boogeyman or some scary figure with a gun. But there are so many crimes committed using nothing more than a phone or an Internet connection. It's not the boogeyman we need to fear; it's the people we think are our friends. But Sasha you brought out things in me that I didn't know I could feel. You taught me what love was."

Even though my heart is bursting, I try to rein in my tears. I've spent a long time waiting for the man who could see past the performance I put on for the world and look deeper to who I am inside. This is a time for happiness, not tears.

"You did the same for me, pretty boy. Now get some sleep."

His eyes stay on mine for a long time until he finally falls to sleep. Eventually I drift off too, still holding his hand.

Some things are worth holding on to.

Chapter Seventeen

Gabe

Six weeks later ...

I lean against the wall in The Lounge, Sasha's newly renovated jazz club, and watch the love of my life work the crowd. The last few weeks have been a flurry of activity as she attacked planning her grand opening celebration with renewed energy and vigor. Since I'd paid contractors to build out the space, she'd been able to order furniture and concentrate on hiring servers.

I've been slowly recovering from Blade's attack and things have been quiet. Max has left the country and we're all stuck in a sort of limbo waiting to see what will happen next. Not that I'm taking any chances with Sasha's safety. I told her that she would have a permanent shadow for the rest of her natural life whether she wants one or not.

When I stand up straighter, my side aches slightly. My injury made it difficult for me to help Sasha as much as I wanted to. Although I'd offered more financial help, she'd declined. When I'd finally come to visit the club and seen the expensive furniture and light fixtures that she'd had installed, I'd been worried that she was putting herself into debt to finance it all.

With a secretive little smile, she'd opened her laptop and pulled up a website. On the screen was a video entitled "Falling Hard / Failing Hard REMIX." We've had several conversations about how her moment of humiliation has affected her life. She told me about how for months her family wasn't even allowed to *mention* the name of the show. So I was shocked that she wanted me to actually watch the video.

"Sasha, what is this?"

She hit play on the video and after an advertisement was shown, the video of her audition played. It had been overlaid with an auto-tuned remix of the song. At the part where she falls and her skirt flips up, the video has it on a loop so she's shown falling over and over again while her own voice sings "Falling hard, Falling-Falling-Hard." Her exposed bottom is stamped with the words #EpicFAIL.

The way it was edited actually made it even funnier.

Before I could stop myself I laughed. Horrified, I clapped a hand over my mouth only to look over and see that Sasha was laughing, too. So hard she had tears in her eyes.

"Either you are really well-adjusted or there's something I'm missing. Sasha, whoever did this has made this video even more popular than it was before. You'll never be able to get away from it.

Look at the views!" The video had been played more than a million times.

Sasha grinned and pointed to the screen. I peered closer and that's when I noticed the user name of the person who uploaded the video. *SashaSass*. I looked over at her in astonishment.

"That's right, pretty boy. Every time those haters click on this to laugh at me, I'm getting ad revenue. They can laugh but they're paying for my club!"

There's a sudden roar from the crowd in the club and I look up to see that Sasha's on stage. The music starts from her now infamous single "Falling Hard - Failing Hard." Her remix of the original song was so popular that she's now working on a full-length album. She's determined to do it her way: sassy, sexy and jazz-inspired. The crowd sings along with the chorus and when she reaches the end, she flips up her skirt playfully to reveal yellow polka-dot shorts.

I laugh along with everyone else. Sasha giggles and then turns the mic over to the next act. As soon as she comes off the stage, I'm there to meet her. She accepts my hand and then hugs me gently.

"Sasha! You were amazing."

We turn to see her sisters. Sasha squeals and before long she's in the middle of a big, messy group hug. It took time for her family to come around but once they saw Sasha's enthusiasm and her incredible savvy, they started taking her more seriously. No matter how strong she is I know that having her family in her corner means the world to her.

"Congratulations, sis. You really did it. This place is great. And

Dad is over the moon."

Her sister Audra points across the room to where Sasha's parents stand at the bar. Her father has a faraway look on his face. I know he's in a good place tonight because he didn't give me too much hell when I talked to him earlier. Although the fact that I was asking for his permission to ask for Sasha's hand in marriage probably went a long way toward his being so friendly.

After my hasty marriage proposal, I never mentioned it again. My sweet girl hasn't brought it up either. I think she has assumed that I was so out of it that I don't remember the conversation. Nothing could be further from the truth. I just want her to have everything. Including a proper proposal from a man who doesn't look like he's at death's door.

I pat my pocket nervously. I'm not going to do it here. This is Sasha's moment. Pride swells as I watch her shake hands with her producer and several of the artists who have performed tonight. Just like I told her she would on the roof that night, she's finally found her place.

And even in a room full of stars, she's shining the brightest of all.

* * * * *

When we arrive home that night, Sasha does the same thing she always does: drop her handbag and slip out of her shoes. I follow her upstairs and then wait until she's changed into a nightshirt and shorts for bed. I strip down to my boxers, gripping the ring box in my hand. Once I slide under the covers, I move over so she can rest her head on my shoulder. Her hand plays with my hair idly and I have to smile.

Unconsciously she's mirroring everything we did that night.

"I'm so sorry. So sorry, beautiful girl."

Her nose crinkles in surprise. "What do you mean? Sorry for what?"

I lift her hand to my lips and kiss the tips of her fingers. "I know you don't like the idea of just living together. You're a *good girl*."

She stares at me, perplexed. I can see the moment that she figures out what's going on. Her eyes drop to my other hand, clenched into a fist resting at my side. She gasps and her eyes dart back to mine, searching.

I squeeze her fingers, looking deep into her eyes. "And I love that about you. So let's get married."

"Oh my god. I didn't think you remembered." She pulls me in for a soft, lingering kiss. Then just like last time, she plants a little kiss on the tip of my nose. "*Yes*. I still think you're loopy."

"No, I'm just in love." Then I proceed to show her just how much I love her. I can't put my usual moves on her considering how stiff I still am but I'm more than willing to let her be the strong, in charge woman I know she is. A while later, she collapses next to me, panting almost as hard as I am.

She lets out a little sigh. "Oh Gabe. I guess charming isn't so bad sometimes."

"Sasha? I want to tell you something."

After she's caught her breath, I turn my head until my lips brush her forehead.

"I made a promise to Zack not to be a criminal. But *you* are the one who makes me want to be a good person. I'm not worthy of you but I'm going to spend every day trying to be the kind of guy you deserve. A good guy."

"Not too good I hope. You know I like bad boys," she teases.

"For you, I'll always be as bad as you want me to be."

The End

You just finished reading the third book in the Blue-Collar Billionaires series. Stay tuned for a special excerpt of the previous book in the series, **FINN**.

Did you miss the previous book?

~ *FINN (Blue-Collar Billionaires #2)* ~

is available now!

Finn Marshall survived several tours in Afghanistan before the billionaire father he barely remembers changed everything. Now he has it all: money, cars and most importantly, power. Power to track down the woman who left him for a richer man.

Marissa dragged herself out of poverty one client at a time, so she's thrilled when her company, Maid-4-U, gets a huge contract for a luxury penthouse. Until she sees who owns it.

Now to save her struggling business, Finn demands everything she once promised him. Money can't buy him happiness but it can buy him one thing: REVENGE

EXCERPT of *FINN (Blue-Collar Billionaires #2)*
© August 2014 M. Malone

RISSA

My fingers curl around the tight band of my pencil skirt. Usually I'm wearing the same basic uniform as the rest of the maids, casual clothing covered by a green and yellow Maid-4-U apron that Daphne designed for us last year. But today, I'm here to bring the signed contract to the client and see the area we'll be working in. I have to look professional. Put together.

I swallow against a wave of nerves and run my hands over my hair again. The unruly red curls tend to have a mind of their own so I've pulled them back into a low bun. I can't screw up this job. This could be the start of a whole new wave of luck for our business. Daphne is the optimist, but secretly I'm starting to agree with her that this new deal is a sign.

Our luck is finally changing.

After my moment of self-reflection, I walk into the lobby. It's not as impressive as I imagined it would be. Considering the amount of money we've been offered to clean this place, I was expecting solid gold floors and diamond encrusted door handles. But it's just a plain entryway painted builder white.

There's a man behind the counter. I nod at him and then take a seat on one of the couches in the waiting area. Mr. Stevens is supposed to meet me here and take me up so I can see the property and meet the owner. After about ten minutes, I pull out my cell phone. Where is he?

What is it with rich people? They always think everyone else should be on their timetable. It makes me think about Andrew. He'd done this type of thing often. He would rush me along but consistently show up late or not at all when I needed him. The only time he'd really shown emotion was anytime someone mentioned my relationship with Finn.

I close my eyes.

Even now years later just the thought of him is enough to bring tears to my eyes. *My sweet, Finn*. His family lived in the same trailer park and we'd shared the experience of being the trash from the wrong side of the tracks at our school. He'd been my first kiss, my first love. My first everything. Then after school he'd gone off to the army and things had never been the same.

I'm suddenly pulled from my thoughts by the sound of my name. The man behind the front desk is standing now, peering at me with interest. "Miss Blake?"

"Yes, that's me."

"Mr. Stevens just called. He told me to let you up immediately." He stands and walks to the elevator. I follow him on and then watch as he inserts a key from the massive ring in his hand. He twists it and then punches the button for the twelfth floor. I watch in surprise as he steps back out. The doors close behind me and the elevator hurtles upward.

The nerves I felt downstairs come back full force when the doors open with a ding. I step out of the elevator and into a hallway. There are doors at the end of the hallway in both directions. I let out a little sigh. It all seems a little rude, to summon me up here but not have anyone waiting to show me where to go.

I look down the hallway to my left. The door to 15B is partially open. *That must be it, then.* I walk down the hall, my feet sinking into the deep luxurious carpet. When I push open the door, it doesn't make a sound.

"Hello?"

I walk inside and then stop in awe. It's so beautiful. I never even knew that apartments like this existed in Norfolk. The ceilings are much higher than normal. I estimate that they must be at least fifteen feet high. The room I'm standing in has two large, deeply stuffed couches angled to face the windows. To my left is a beautiful gourmet kitchen with tall, cherry cabinets and gleaming stainless steel appliances. There's a hallway to the side that must lead to the bedrooms.

I'm going to be working here? As I look around in wonder, I have to ask why the owner even hired me. The place looks pristine already.

There must be some mistake. Maybe the owner just wanted to meet here so we could talk about the contract before he shows me the apartments in the building that actually need cleaning. But even still, I'm sure the other apartments in the building must be lovely, too.

"Hello? Sir?"

It hits me then that I don't even know the owner's name. Mr. Stevens has been my contact throughout this entire process and although there was a company name on the contract, I didn't even think to ask the name of the representative the company would be sending over.

"Do you like the view?"

The deep voice comes from the shadows of the hallway. Even though I just called out for someone, it startles me. And all at once, it reminds me that there's no one else here. When I agreed to this meeting, it was under the assumption that Mr. Stevens would be present as well. But now I'm alone with some man that I've never met.

A man with a voice that's both haunting and terrifying.

"I do. This is a beautiful place," I answer, hoping that he'll come out from the hallway so I can see what he looks like.

I really hope he's not creepy or some kind of jerk, the way Tara thought. But even if he is, I'll have to deal with it because we can't afford to lose this contract.

"I bought it just this year. I enjoy surrounding myself with beautiful things."

His words are strangely inappropriate yet I'm enthralled. I should be angling closer to the door so I can get the hell out of here if he does anything weird. But I can't move. There's something about his voice. The way he speaks. It's familiar and heartbreaking all at once.

"You pulled your hair back. Hair like yours should never be restrained."

Even before he steps forward, my traitorous heart skips a beat. How could I ever forget that voice, the voice that promised me that I'd never be alone, that he'd always be there? That we'd be a team. The voice that told me I was everything before I was foolish enough to throw it all away.

"Finn?"

THE ALEXANDERS

~ EBOOKS AVAILABLE ~

BLUE-COLLAR BILLIONAIRES

~ EBOOKS AVAILABLE ~

 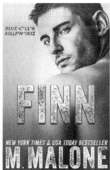 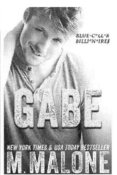

~ COMING SOON ~

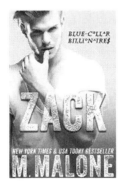 

PRINT BOOKS AVAILABLE

THE ALEXANDERS

Book 1 - *One More Day* ~ Jackson + Ridley
(contains Book 0.5 - *Teasing Trent: the prequel*)

Book 2 - *The Things I Do for You* ~ Nick + Raina

Book 3 - *He's the Man* ~ Matt + Penny

Book 4 - *All I Need is You* ~ Eli + Kay
(contains Book 3.5 - *Christmas with The Alexanders*)

Book 5 - *Say You Will* ~ Trent + Mara

BLUE-COLLAR BILLIONAIRES

Book 1 - TANK
Book 2 – FINN
Book 3 – GABE

coming soon
Book 4 – ZACK
Book 4 - LUKE

ABOUT THE AUTHOR

New York Times & *USA TODAY* Bestselling author M. Malone lives in the Washington, D.C. metro area with her three favorite guys: her husband and their two sons. She likes dramatic opera music, staid old men wearing suspenders, claw-foot bathtubs, and unexpected surprises.

The thing she likes best is getting to make up stuff for a living.

www.MMaloneBooks.com

Made in the USA
Middletown, DE
04 January 2019